Based on a True Story

To God, the One who is always with me

To Dad, blood is thicker than water. #iamawriter

To Mom, Valuable and valued.

To Jay, connected and committed to you.

To Shemaya, *Numero Uno.*

Thanks to all who helped proofread Entangled. I really appreciate your support:

1. *Joycelyn Igiri*
2. *Daniel & Xolase Ayittey*
3. *Chidi & Ijeoma Ukandu*
4. *Dorcas Sina-Olulana*
5. *Korkor Korletey-Sackey*

Acknowledging Josh Seas for the Photos

Entangled in a web of women,

I did not know how strong the strings were

Until I had to choose one of them.

I felt always young, yet was growing older

It was inevitable. I realized that at some point

I could no longer remain ... Single

This page is Intentionally left blank

A Friendly Gesture

"Do not be one of those who shakes hands in a pledge,
One of those who is surety for debts;" Proverbs 22:26

"Hello..."

"Hi Philip! It's me, Hassan. Hassan Garba, Methodist Boys"

"Wow! Great to hear from you. How have you been?"

"I am doing well Philip. But I hear you are doing much better. How is Accra?"

"Ha ha ha ha. I see word has travelled quickly."

"Of course. Good news travels fast. How is your new place? I hear there is regular power... what a refreshing experience it must be."

"Ha ha ha... Hassan truly I say unto you, we have power 25 by 8!"

Both men burst out laughing. Philip and Hassan had been fellow prefects at Methodist Boys' High School, Lagos Nigeria. They had not been very close for a while, but Philip was on good terms with everyone and Hassan felt comfortable calling him to say hello and ask a favour. Philip was approachable. He somehow always felt the need to lend a helping hand whenever he could to whoever needed such help. Kind-hearted or people-pleaser, you could choose what you wanted to call him; maybe even phlegmatic or just plain naïve. Whatever you chose to call him, that was just the way he was and those around him knew.

Philip Ezeani had just moved to Accra. A plum job with a Graphic Arts company was the result of months of prayer. His Facebook profile location change made a month or so previously had triggered a plethora of congratulatory messages not to mention requests for assistance. The resumes, the questions about what Accra was like, the requests for airport pickups and on and on. He always helped except when it was really not convenient for him. Philip loved two things most in life: God and work. He loved his family too somewhere in between those two.

Hassan continued. He chose to speak to Philip in Pidgin English, probably an effort to engage more intimately.

"Phil e get wetin I wan ask you o"

"Go ahead."

Philip understood Pidgin English well, but he was not so good at it. Some people considered him very British in his behaviour and command of the English language. He did not have the Welsh slur though, but he seemed to pronounce every word correctly, as all the major dictionaries prescribed. He mostly responded in *correct* English whatever brand of English was spoken to him.

"My cousin wan come do masters for Ghana. I been think say she fit perch with you for one week. After that she go get her own place..."

"She? She is a girl?"

"Ah. Philip no cause for alarm. She be correct girl. No problem. And she dey go church well so..."

"She goes to church?"

"Yes Sir"

"But she is your cousin?"

"Yes. Her father is a Christian. She is a very serious Christian herself. You know say my family na big family. Some of us are Muslims but some are Christians. But she is my cousin and I know her well."

Philip took it all in with a pinch of salt. A Muslim Hassan with a Christian cousin who wants to stay with a strange man in Accra. Alarms went off in Philip's mind. He was living alone in a three bedroom, fully furnished flat in faraway Accra doing his very best to keep aggressive young ladies away from his middle-aged body not to mention his house and car. It was more precarious because he had spent most of his early adult years teaching young people that an unmarried couple should not live together under any circumstance.

Hassan knew Philip was a Christian. He knew some Christians did not sleep with girls before they were married. He also knew some did. Besides, he did not really believe Philip had not slept with a girl at thirty-three. That was in no way possible in the twenty-first century. It was difficult to believe even with a Catholic Priest! Besides, it was a good deal if at some point Philip found that he liked Zainab and wanted to marry her. He was rich, a Christian and a great person to have as an in-law.

And why would such thoughts cross Hassan's mind? Maybe because most people who belong to one Church or the other give the impression that more things are permissible than actually are. After all, there is no verse in the Bible that explicitly states that living with a lady is wrong, or even fondling or kissing her. After all, avoiding fornication as the Bible prescribes does not mean one cannot sleep on the same bed with a lady, does it?

"Hassan, you know I am a Christian..."

"Oh, Philip I know now. I tell you say she be Christian too. She is a nice girl o, there is no cause for alarm. "

"Hassan, I am not so sure..."

"Philip, it is only for one-week na. She will be OK. In fact, I should have told you; she already has a place, it is just that they want to do some repairs in the house which will only take a few days. You know these landlords. It is just like in Nigeria. They want to use people's money to complete their houses!"

"So why does she not get somewhere else?"

"Bros... you know now. The place is close to the school and it is students' price..."

"OK. Hassan. Let's do this. Can you call me back later in the evening after work, so we can talk more about this?"

"OK. No problem bros. Thank you so much. I am counting on you ooo"

"Alright. Later then"

"OK. Have a great day. No forget us in your kingdom o"

Philip dropped the call. He paused a few seconds and stared at the clock. A few minutes after seven o'clock. He had spoken to Hassan for almost fifteen minutes. He looked back at the bed, unkempt as usual. He would leave it that way till he was ready to use it again. No one was watching after all. No one? He hurriedly tucked a few parts in and spread the blanket out neatly. He dashed to the wardrobe and pulled out a pair of boxers and a vest. In twenty minutes he was out of the bathroom, still thinking about the discussion with Hassan.

Why was the decision difficult? It could have been sorted out with a simple 'NO' but Philip was not one to say 'NO' too often, he would rather inconvenience himself than someone else.

FLIRT

The office was busy as usual. Philip filled up every minute of the day with something useful to the company or useful to himself. Social media were completely out of the question during work hours. As friendly as he was, he hardly paid attention to office chat between 8:00 AM and 6:00 PM except some went out of their way to speak directly to him. Once in a while a specific person did: Helen Eduful. She was Fante. The Fante tribe was arguably the most sophisticated of Ghana's top four tribes. The Fantes were considered to have fraternized most with the Europeans in the colonial era. The mid-morning tea tradition could still be observed among elderly women living in remote villages. Fante single ladies were often the high fliers in the corporate world. Philip Ezeani was strongly attracted to high-flying, aggressive women.

Helen was outgoing, intelligent, and popular in the office environment. She did not have the wide hips typical of certain Akans and Krobos; neither would she particularly appear in the top five runners-up in a Miss Ghana pageant but her high shoulders, tidy bust, flat tummy and spotless finesse with spoken English made her very attractive. She happened to choose Philip as her 'Office Husband'. She called him '*Husby*'. Philip did not call her Wify but he did not object to being called by the suggestive name.

"Husby, Eti seyin[1]?" she started with a giggle, breaking into Philip's thoughts. He was not really in the mood for a chat, but he could not ignore her.

"ɛyɛ[2]", he responded, staring at his laptop screen for a few more seconds before turning to her. She giggled harder.

"You are improving o," she placed her left hand on his shoulder, "Aren't you going for lunch? It is past one o'clock"

---

[1] Twi for 'How are you?'
[2] Twi for 'Fine'

"O... is it? Are you ready to go?"

"Yup. Would you like to come keep your *wify* company?"

"Ha ha ha ha ha..."

Philip tidied up a bit. He rose slowly while locking his screen and ignoring a few glances from his colleagues. In a minute he was stepping out of the glass cubicle built for four. Helen took the liberty of hanging her left hand on his right forearm, chatty as ever.

Lunch was the usual. No one was ever happy with the idea of having to stand in line for food even if it was for just a few minutes. Variants of Rice; Banku with Tilapia and Fufu stared at Philip and Helen from the serving tables.

"What are you having?" asked Helen.

"Oh. Jollof... what else is there?"

"Oh, you are so boring...," laughed Helen "Try the Fufu or Banku. Don't be so unadventurous"

"Unadventurous. Ha Ha. Please let me be safe. Besides, I do not like eating with my hands in public"

Helen roared with laughter.

"Self-consciousness. Who is looking at you? Your numerous girlfriends eh?"

"Ha ha ha. I don't have any ooo. It's just that I do not want that smell of whatever "swallow" it is on my hands..."

"What! But you can wash your hands now."

"One wash never does enough cleaning"

"I hear you. So, you have a bath after each meal at home, right?"

Philip almost hit the lady behind him laughing. Eyes were on them. Most of their colleagues had noticed the brewing love affair between 'those two'. Helen chuckled easily with almost any man but there was something special about the connection with Philip. It could be the Nigerian-ness, the thought of being with a foreigner, the adventure of something different. Helen loved adventure, the sanguine in her was strong ever seeking new thrills and often getting them. Philip on the other hand was never too sure what to make of their friendship. Would it be a nice idea to ask her out? It was typical of him to be very hesitant with relationships anyway: the perfect melancholy. He had never been too sure what a woman's advances really meant. In the past, he had often come to the wrong conclusions or maybe he had just concluded too soon or even concluded wrongly.

Philip Ezeani was not a flirt but he was very good with ladies and they loved being with him. Who wouldn't love a well-behaved, well-spoken, intelligent, rich young man. Some had concluded he didn't know what he wanted in a woman simply because he did not want them or could not make up his mind whether he wanted them. Maybe they were right. What did he really want? At thirty plus, he had never really successfully defined a relationship with a lady as a romantic one. Maybe he could have made a strong flirt if his humanity had been more pronounced than his Christianity.

About six pm Philip got another call from Hassan. He had to ask him to call back. "I am driving... can we talk later this night? About 10:00 PM?" He still wasn't sure of the answer he would give. Was he going to let a lady stay at his place for a week? How would he explain that to the numerous 'disciples' he had raised back on campus if someone in Nigeria heard? Even if nothing happened, it would still seem an *appearance of evil,* wouldn't it? The neighbours would see, and tongues would wag. He had never preached to them, but they must have heard his late-night prayers during his weekends. Besides, he almost never missed Sunday and Wednesday services. They knew he was at least somewhat serious with his faith unlike most rich young men. They probably wondered how come he often kept such late nights ... safer to be with ladies in public?

"Penny for your thoughts?" asked Abena.

"I am Pan-African!"

"What?"

"I do not take foreign currencies..."

"Nonsense. You think I do not know you are paid in dollars. Ha ha... what are you so lost in thought about, don't try to dodge the question."

"Nothing serious"

"Out with it. What are friends for?"

Philip paused a bit while taking a left turn at the National Arts Theatre headed straight for *Afia African Village* on the outskirts of North Ridge. He had been introduced to Abena by a colleague. She worked at a bank a few blocks from his office and they got along quite well. She was the go-getter type, very smart and serious minded, never giving away her emotions. At thirty-one she did not seem particularly bothered about marriage and relationships and as far as Philip was concerned she was satisfied being a good friend.

Once in a while they spent time eating out after work. It was often spontaneous. Philip had some unexplainable spontaneity about him and whenever he asked she never said 'no'. She lived alone like himself and was never in any particular hurry to go home after work. Neither of them ever really thought about those outings as a date... another undefined relationship for Philip; good company for Abena Adjei-Antwi.

"One of my friends in Nigeria wants me to host his cousin for a week..."

"OK. And?"

"She is a lady..."

"Ohhh... I see. He is sending you a wife..." She looked out the window and smiled mischievously. Philip glanced at her from the corner of his right eye trying to interpret the look on her face:

surprise? Jealousy? Disgust? Joy? He could not tell. He often considered himself some sort of pseudo-psychic or prophet, able to *discern* people's feelings and personalities just from the look on their faces. There were some people he simply could not read. He was fascinated with such people and felt even more drawn to them especially when they were ladies. The marriage issue was something he often avoided. He hardly encouraged conversation in that direction though he thought about it a lot as he did Amarachi Onuoma. He applied one last burst of force on the accelerator as they approached Afia, an expression of the turmoil his memories had brewed in his soul momentarily.

They both stepped out of the car. It was a Volkswagen Touareg. He had to help her step down, she still being in her heels. The SUV was about a foot higher than the floor. She held on to his hand as they walked into the lounge. The off-white lights were warm. Both stopped momentarily to smile back at the ladies at the reception. Had he been alone, he would have chatted a while, but he had some respect for the lady he was with whenever he was with one. They helped themselves to a soft double couch still holding hands. A few other couples were sitting around drinking and chatting in the lounge. They could feel the breeze from the beach beside which Afia stood. The breeze was so tempting. He imagined cuddling up in a soft chair with someone.

"So, what would you like?" Philip asked

"What are you having?"

"Oh, for me it is always pineapple juice. Theirs is nice. I have one every now and then"

"So how often do you come here?"

"Oh, not very often. I come when I need a quiet place to retreat to. There are other places though. I prefer quiet outings any day. Have you been to Weija Dam?"

"Nope"

"Great place too. You could take a good book there and just relax a Saturday afternoon away"

"I see. So, who do you go with?"

Abena gave him a certain look. She made a face that told Philip it was not really a serious question, but he wanted to answer it seriously anyway. He never liked being perceived as some player.

"Often alone," he smiled.

"I see" Abena looked around at the other couples in the lounge. There was a group of white young people just outside the lounge. Afia had a sitting area made of very hard wood just outside the lounge facing the ocean. Beside this was a wooden staircase that led to a narrow walkway which ended up at the seaside. The beach was lovely: summer hats, palm trees and pure white sand. A barricade cordoned off the ocean itself and one had to open a small gate to get a feel of the mighty white ocean itself. Sitting around a summer hat and feeling the breeze was enough for most people. Each summer hat had a dim light bulb which exposed only silhouettes of holiday makers in a variety of outfits ranging from bikinis to blue jeans and T-shirts.

"Would you like to come with me sometime?" Philip asked, breaking into Abena's thoughts but not looking at her.

"Of course," answered Abena "... you know it is amazing the number of spots you know in Accra. Who takes you to all these places?"

Philip burst out laughing. If he didn't know better, he would have concluded that Abena was getting very curious about his personal life and other ladies in his life lately. Was it interest or just curiosity? It would not be farfetched if it ended up being interest. It had happened before; more than once or twice. He meets a lady and assumes she is just a friend then over a few months he is no longer sure where the lines are, the lady is dying for him to make a move, but he is not so sure what to do next.

11:00 PM. It was time to call Hassan Garba. It had been a long night. He had dropped Abena off by 10:30 PM. Night driving in Accra was not as dangerous as it would have been in Lagos. Philip never drove in Lagos, at least not his own car. The job had been a breakthrough for him but it was yet unclear whether it was a blessing or a curse giving the trend of things. Some say you cannot claim to be an honest person till you have been exposed to opportunities for theft. Philip had never lived alone so he could not say he was really faithful at keeping himself pure for God. He had never been in a relationship so he could not claim to have enough self-control to see the same woman daily and not have sex with her. He had never been this rich, so he could not now tell what the motives of the growing harem of "virgins" were.

A virgin at thirty plus... impressive some may think for a man. As he made the last right turn leading to his three-bedroom flat he recalled his conversation he had had with Bose, a plump young lady whose number he had lifted from the third page of The Sun Newspaper back in Nigeria. He had a knack for chatting with ladies on social media. It seemed a safe distance from real danger. Actually, calling them was not so common but he called Bose; it was one of those adventure days. She was a member of *The Called Out Church*, a prominent charismatic church in Lagos and she claimed to be in the work force. He was surprised how hysterically she had laughed when he told her he was a virgin at twenty-six. More than five years later, he was still a virgin. Impressive; impressive to man but not necessarily to God.

Philip enjoyed the tranquil nature of his neighbourhood, particularly in the evenings though he hardly ever got to really enjoy it. As he stepped out of his car to open the gate, that lonely feeling came again. He was again going to step into an empty three-bedroom flat. Maybe he would call his fellow night crawler, Emem Allen-Howard. What time would it be in Port Harcourt right then?

Midnight? Whatever time it was, she always picked his calls and she could be wide awake till 2:00 AM.

"Hassan. How are you?"

"..." Hassan must have been asleep for two hours. He pulled himself up on the bed. After all, the discussion was more beneficial to him than to his expatriate friend.

"Am fine," he finally answered.

"So, About Zainab. I really don't think..."

"Bros why you dey do me like this now? Make you help person small na... I say make you just help me for one week, only one week..."

"Hassan, you don't have to interrupt me. I have my reasons for my response. It is not personal"

"Philip no be say I dey vex for you but you suppose understand say before I call you I know say you be correct Church boy. Na condition cause this matter. I no wan make Zainab lose this opportunity. You know say that side no dey like Nigerian schools. If she no come on time she fit miss something."

Philip had his reasons. He had taught many that it was not healthy to live with the opposite sex in the same house. It was not safe to stay overnight or behind closed doors with a lady... the thoughts rang through his head. Was the situation peculiar or was he just being overcome by his desire to please others. He felt he needed to yield and let Zainab come. He needed the company and what could possibly happen in a week?

"OK," he finally consented, interrupting Hassan's ranting.

"Sorry?"

"I said OK. When is she coming?"

"Wow... thanks very much. I appreciate. God bless you Sir. You will not regret it. She is a very nice girl. She will behave..."

"Yeah, yeah... I hear you"

"Thanks Bros. She will be there in like two weeks. Last week of June"

"OK. Just keep in touch. "

"No wahala. Abeg bros make I sleep small... thank you plenty"

"Alright. Have a good night"

"God bless..."

Philip Ezeani what are you doing? It was as silent as midnight in Accra. Crickets could be heard chirping loudly but the alarm bells that rang in Philip's inner being were loud enough to keep him awake for another thirty minutes. How would he make the rules? No shorts outside the room? No towels outside the bathroom? No touching in the evening? How was he possibly going to live in the same house with a lady and not lose control? Wait a minute? Was she even a Christian? Zainab! She was probably a Moslem like her cousin. At least some of them had good morals. If he didn't start anything she probably would not. Or would she?

He remembered Efe and Harriet. They had worked together back in the day during his National Youth Service year. Shortly after they began work, they had proposed staying together in a three bedroom flat. Everyone would have their room and they would all share the living room, kitchen and bathroom. It sounded pragmatic, but his conscience would not allow. What could happen with two women in the house? What could not happen? It seems some moral lines blur as one got older, or is it as one got richer? Or more exposed to the wider world. He had accepted. Zainab was coming. He was going to live with her for a week. A week alone with a woman in the house. He had seen her once and wasn't so attracted so it still felt safe. Nothing would happen!

"Are you afraid we will rape you?" Harriet had joked back then. She was the bubbly, outgoing one of the two. Efe just joined in the laughter. Philip couldn't say why because they would not understand. They were both Christians too but did not really mind staying in the same house with a man. They had probably done it before back in University of Port Harcourt without batting an eyelid.

"It is like you have a lot of money," Harriet ventured again, driving her argument harder.

"Philip why now? You don't want to stay with us? This is the cheaper option o"

All efforts to extract the reasons for his refusal failed. Their manager had earlier proposed that the company could pay for a joint accommodation for three of them if they could find a place. He had not budged. His answer was final. Possibly the fire of campus fellowship was still burning bright. His answer was "NO". His answer had changed in Accra. This time it was only one lady.

Friends at First Sight

"Can a man take fire to his bosom,
And his clothes not be burned?" Proverbs 6:27

Spontaneity. It was not unusual for Philip to suddenly become friendly with total strangers. Once in while he met someone that simply had that inexplicable magical spark that connected with him. Jokes would become absolutely natural and flow flawlessly. The dialogue as it often was would spiral from one subject to another till someone or something broke it. His melancholy in private could not be reconciled with his sporadic expressions of sanguine behaviour. It was even more pronounced when the other party drove the conversion. The other party was often a lady, middle-aged, young, married, single, pretty, not-so-pretty, it didn't matter! What mattered was the spark.

Gazelle West Africa had built a reputation for comfortable bus transport across the region. Their eight to ten-hour drives from Lagos to Accra were the viable alternative for those who had class but could not afford a flight ticket or simply wanted to enjoy the West African Coastline. Zainab had the spark. She glowed right from the time she stepped off the bus. Five feet seven. Flawless dark skin. Perfectly shaped set of teeth. When she smiled her eyes glowed and she exposed them: dazzling white. She wore a TM Shirt with thick lilac stripes. It looked quite new. She definitely looked slightly improved when compared with the picture in Philip's memory. He previously thought he would not really be attracted to her part of his reason for letting this arrangement happen. She spotted him from afar. He was always more popular than he thought. People knew him from afar that he did not know growing up. Zainab knew him and smiled brightly.

She stepped down from the bus, dragging along her hand luggage and saying goodbye to friends she had made on the bus. Philip approached her, blushing, unable to take away the smile from his face till it became like plastic. "Oh, nothing will happen" he thought to himself. Once close enough she hugged him and held on for about three seconds.

"Oh Philip. Thank you so much. It's so good to see you"

Philip hesitated but did not want to seem archaic. He held on to her lightly and responded as much as he could. He recalled that question a friend had asked him back in secondary school: 'why do you startle so much when a girl touches you?'. What was the answer again?

"Good to see you too... ", Philip responded after a short lag.

Zainab leaned back and smiled again. It could have disarmed a Russian soldier. Philip glanced at the yellow handbag dangling from her left arm while looking for something else to focus on asides Zainab's face. She broke the brief silence.

"Please come help me with my big box"

"OK"

Her hand slithered down his upper arm and back to her hand luggage as they both went back to the ninety-seater luxury bus. It was rowdy. Passengers were clamouring for their luggage while the bus conductors did their best to help maintain sanity. Zainab stayed an inch behind Philip pointing out her huge brown leather bag. It was out in a few minutes after just a little pushing and shoving and both walked side by side out of the park to the busy highway where Philip had parked on the covert.

The ride was very chatty. One chatty lady with one responsive man creates a chatty ride in a brand-new city. Much of the conversation was about her experience with the trip and her questions about Ghana.

"... I hate sitting for long..."

"Thank God you made it then. It's not a problem for us..."

"Us?"

"When I was you we used to go home every Christmas like most Igbos. The bus ride is about ten hours..."

"O God!"

"Hahaha"

"I have never travelled like this before. My legs ache eh... annoying"

"Sorry..."

"But I met nice people anyway... Ghanaians are nice..."

"Yes. More civil. More likely to talk to you with respect than the typical Nigerian. Or should I say the typical Lagosian... always in a hurry somewhere"

"Do you blame them?"

"But did you ever go to your home town when you were young?"

"Oh No. To do what in that village? "

"Where do you come from?"

"Kwara..."

"So, you have never been to your village?"

"I don't remember o. But I have been to Ilorin many times with my Dad"

"OK"

"Lights everywhere!"

"Haha..."

"I heard Ghana has not had a power failure in the last ten years..."

"Ghana or Accra? Well I heard that too before I came. It's not perfectly true. Once in a while ECG strikes but it is not so often"

"And the traffic lights even work"

"Haha. But the traffic lights work in Naija too na"

"Where? VI?"

"At least VI and Ikoyi"

They shared their first session of hard laughter. Philip had to face the road, but Zainab leaned sideways looking at him almost throughout the ride. Once or twice she looked out the window when something interesting caught her attention. The road from Gazelle Bus Park through Kwame Nkrumah Circle to Adabraka was not so different from typical Nigerian roads. Circle, as it was popularly called reminded Zainab of Mile 2 back in Lagos. There was nothing so interesting about the city asides the working traffic lights on the road to Accra Central, the plethora of working lights and one or two hotels so Philip was the main attraction so far.

The last five minutes of the ride were somewhat quiet. Maybe the excitement had quelled a bit or the reality that they were going to be sleeping in the same house alone was becoming heavier on both of them. Even for a non-believer in Jesus Christ, sharing a house alone with a man was a bit disconcerting for an African woman more-so when nothing romantic was happening or expected to happen. It was more disturbing for Philip because he did not expect to be attracted to her or enjoy her company like this. He was not prepared for this.

"Let me help with the gate" Zainab ventured once it became obvious that they had arrived.

"Oh no don't worry"

"OK."

She sat and stared a bit then threw her face away as though she was stopping herself from becoming attached.

The neighbourhood was quiet. it was purely residential, and Philip's house was almost at the end of a close with detached bungalows on both sides all the way along the close. Almost every house had a flower bed in front and the walls were ever so short. Not many were concerned about having electric wire or spikes. Apparently, security was not much of an issue in Accra. The peace and quiet of the evening and the lights gave the atmosphere such a subtle sense of romance. It would be great to be married in Accra, wouldn't it?

The gates were open, and Philip was back in the car to drive in. Zainab stepped out once he had come to a complete stop and watched him close the gates. She turned away again and looked towards the carpet grass in front of the apartment. A few green shrubs were also growing along the short wall. She looked around. The house reminded Zainab of Surulere back in Lagos. The houses in this area must have been built about the same time too: the 70s, way before she was born. So much space for just one person.

"Do you stay alone here? "

"Of course,"

"The whole compound?"

"Oh no. There is a BQ. My neighbour lives there with his wife and two kids."

"OK. So, you have the front house to yourself?"

"Yeah"

Another silence ensued as they grappled with the bags. Philip noticed the change in Zainab's voice. When she wasn't excited her voice was so soft, inviting. Philip opened the front door and let her in first, dragging the huge brown bag behind her. He shut the door and turned the key twice as he normally did. His heart missed a beat at the second torque. Zainab giggled.

"What?", Philip asked, half smiling.

"Nothing. Can I use the bathroom?"

"What are you giggling about?"

She laughed.

"You. Such a gentleman! Please the bathroom. I have been holding it back"

"OK. The washroom you mean? Ghanaians say 'washroom'"

"Washroom *ke*? What are they washing there?"

Both roared with laughter.

"This way"

Philip led her passed the kitchen door into the house's main bathroom. She shut the door behind her and he had a moment of silence. He heard the Silent Whisper again: "This is not right". It was quiet again. He never forced his way, he never shouted, he never threatened, he only warned. Ever so silent, the Silent Whisper. 'This is not right'.

He ignored the voice. What could he do now? Send her away? Pay for a hotel room for her? Move to one of his friends' houses? What could he possibly do at this point. Hassan's call broke into his thoughts. He picked up at the second ring. He kept the conversation short, telling him Zainab was in the washroom. He would speak to her early in the morning. Zainab was out in about five minutes. She looked around at the living room again. Light blue walls, almost bare, just a cheap painting hanging over the television which sat on a piece of elaborate furniture specifically designed for electronics. The curtains were rich, blue with some silver patterns all over. She admired them. The floor was very good quality marble with a thick Persian rug at the centre. The large sofa could sit five. It seemed it was a combined piece, made up of one three-seater and a two-seater joined at a ninety-degree angle. Two other chairs leaned adjacent to the door separated by a glass side stool. She walked over to the first chair and sat sinking into the warm chair. Accra seemed a bit cold at night. Philip had turned on the television and she turned her eyes that way after taking a glance at him.

"Your bags... "

"pardon?"

"Let us get your bags in the room" Philip offered.

"OK. Thanks," Another smile formed on Zainab's face.

She wasn't quite sure of what to make of him. He seemed somewhat withdrawn though he made good conversation when spoken to. Did he like her or was he just being nice? He was too nice.

In a few minutes she was out of sight again and Philip was left to his thoughts, his conscience and the Silent Whisper. She had hidden herself in the room to prepare for a shower. Philip walked into his room to undress too. He would normally wear boxer shorts in the house and may or may not wear a shirt. As he pulled down his chino trousers he contemplated how he was going to dress before stepping out. Just then he quickly pulled up his trousers and gently shut his bedroom door. He had forgotten that part of this new arrangement. He could not leave the door open while undressing, could he? He threw his trousers on the bed, hung the shirt by its neck on the open wardrobe door and again promised himself he would get the room tidy when he got back from work the next day. Looking around the room was embarrassing to him while alone. He could not let Zainab see this.

Books which could not fit in the living room shelf piled up by the computer on his desk. Books he *intended* to read. Was he really that busy or was he just very good at moving things to a future date (putting it mildly). The blanket lay across the bed roughly resembling the three-dimensional map of Utopia. A sheet or two lay by the bed next to the wall. The typical routine was to shift things against the wall when it was time to sleep. Those clothes did not move, and that map was not disbanded till it got really bad and the Saturday morning seemed free or when Nana Ama, his non-resident housekeeper came to the rescue once a month or so.

Zainab found her way around her room. It was like a hotel room. Maybe not a five star but a good hotel. Rich blue curtains, closed up shielding her from the reality outside. It suited her personality type, private. She wiped dust off a few really bad areas and decided it would all wait till the next day. She opened the wardrobe, her shirt in hand, paused, sighed and threw it on the bed. Rummaging through her brown box, she pulled out a large towel and wrapped it over her body and walked out of the room to Philip.

"Yes" Philip answered when she knocked on his room door.

"Please can I have a few hangers?"

"Oh OK"

In two seconds the door was open, and he handed her five hangers. He noticed the towel. It was a large one, but he could see the straps of her bra and her smooth thighs. You could almost see a reflection in them. He could not have said much more than "Here..." without stuttering involuntarily. She got a hold of the bunch and turned away back to her room smiling to herself as soon as she turned, holding back a giggle. Philip breathed heavily and began planning how to communicate the House Rules which would include what Zainab could or could not wear. That brought back memories again: the unexpected response from Uduak when he talked to her about the pair of jeans she had been wearing after he just finished preaching to a bunch of students. She had said "You mean that is what you came all the way to tell me?". He had interpreted the response in his mind. He had never asked her about her welfare as her leader but her wearing a pair of jeans had gotten him to engage in a conversation with her that was deeper than "How are you?".

28

He also recalled Uchechi who had threatened to leave the fellowship if he ever spoke to her about the way she dressed again. Even Ngozi, a fellow member of the Fellowship Exco had ranted about his bringing guilt on her when he raised a few issues. "Can you take away guilt like Christ?" she had asked. House Rules were required here but he did not know how Zainab was going to react.

He walked out of the bedroom and just then Zainab was coming out of hers, carrying her shower bag and still clad in a large, white towel. This time there were no bra straps. She walked passed him without saying anything, but she heard his breath and could have felt it ruffle the air across her shoulder. He heard her laugh in the bathroom after turning on the shower.

10:30 PM. It seemed like one of those days Philip preferred would not end too quickly. Local TV was boring as usual. He had never been too enthusiastic about DSTV or maybe it was just another manifestation of his tendency to defer decisions to the near future which always approached very slowly. He surfed a few stations and then let it rest on a late-night movie half considering his planned dialogue with Zainab. She walked into the living room and sat next to him clad in her jeans shorts and a black vest. She leaned forward with her elbows on her thighs, shoulders square. She turned to him without moving her torso.

"What's on TV?"

"Movie..."

"... Do you have any series?"

"Series?"

She ran her fingers through her hair. Some sort of panacea for her tense feeling of discomfort.

"Like Desperate Housewives, Prison Break, Fringe ..."

"I really don't like series. You have to keep anticipating the next episode. I prefer to just watch a full movie and end it there"

"Hahaha. I see. I have Fringe here."

She did not wait for an answer. She sprang up and was back in three minutes with a DVD. She knelt in front of the DVD player and got the disc spinning oblivious of her back which had become positioned in Philip's line of sight. He struggled to focus on something else. Back on her seat beside him, Philip ventured:

"I think we need to make some rules..."

Zainab's heart skipped a beat. She had begun to get comfortable. What rules? She was not one to be restricted. Her freedom was precious. "House Rules" sounded like someone was about to "mother" her all over again. Philip could have started with the line 'You know I am a Christian ...' but he reconsidered. He did not want to sound religious. He just wanted to keep safe from harm. Besides, he had already agreed to have her sleep in his house for a week so being a *Christian* at this point was a little late.

"I think, " he continued, "we need to agree that while you are here, for my sake you kind of watch your dressing..."

The most unexpected thing happened. Zainab burst out laughing. Philip was used to being scolded or ignored when he raised such issues but not being laughed at. She did not stop laughing for a while.

"What? Am I tempting you?"

"I am serious"

She sat her chin on the back of her right hand while her elbow stood on her bare smooth lap. Half mocking, she asked:

"So, what would you like me to wear? Hijab?"

Philip burst out laughing himself.

"No. Just something moderate. Like trousers in the house not shorts."

"OK."

"And I prefer a t-shirt not sleeveless vests"

"OK"

"I do not play secular music in the house either, so you can use earphones..."

"OK. But we can watch secular movies, right?"

Philip paused. Secular movies but no secular music. The *no secular music* rule was something he had become accustomed to since he became a Christian about twenty years earlier. It was sacrosanct. The rule could not be changed. *No secular music.* Strange thing is the movies never seemed to go away. No secular music but 'yes secular movies'.

"Yeah..." he finally answered, doubting himself.

"The ten Commandments minus seven"

Philip chuckled. Zainab did have a witty sense of humour. She was a deep thinker too like all melancholies or their variants. Like Philip.

"It is just to keep safe"

Bed time was less than an hour away. One and a half episodes of Fringe and the time was up. Philip sat up for a for a few minutes and thought about his day. Would he really survive a week at this rate? Was she deliberately trying to get him? Was this some arrangement Hassan had made to mock the Christian faith? Or was it something he should simply enjoy while keeping within the boundaries of purity? He heard what he thought could be Cece Winan's songs playing from Zainab's room. She was a Muslim, wasn't she?

The song woke him up by 4:30 AM. His regular alarm time was about 5:00 AM and even then, he would doze on the bed for another fifteen minutes or so. This morning was special. He had a new life, someone was in the house. Excitement had a way of taking away sleep; something to wake up to. It was a song from Cece Winan's Throne Room and it was coming from Zainab's room. The other significant sounds that morning were the loud prayers from the primary school nearby and the Imam's voice over a megaphone who had just rounded off his own prayers. Zainab was playing Cece Winans. Philip was curious. Did she just like the music or was she some secret disciple? He craved the experience of walking into a woman's room at the early hours of the morning or maybe even waking up in such a woman's arms. He craved what was not his: Zainab. Fifteen minutes passed, and he was still musing. Would praying the morning prayer be hypocritical in this situation? What would it be like to knock on her door? Was she really awake? One would have thought she would be very tired. Another five minutes and he heard a knock on the door. it was a bit startling, unexpected. He sat up and answered:

"Zainab?"

"Yeah..."

"Good morning..."

Philip greeted kind of expecting her to say what she wanted. Part of him was a bit scared, he could hear in his head. Was this some seduction attempt? When younger he often imagined himself as a viable candidate for elaborate attempts by desperate women. God had somehow saved him from such.

"Good morning, Philip..."

Uncle Charles used to say that 'Good morning' wasn't a greeting, it was merely a wish. A few seconds were again consumed in his musing and Zainab broke the silence again:

"Are you awake?"

"Yes, I am"

He pulled himself off the bed, turned on the light, slipped on a t-shirt and opened the door slightly. Zainab was wide awake. She held up a copy of *Our Daily Manner* and smiled. She had her off-white pyjamas dotted with hot pink bougainvillea. She dealt with its translucence by tying a wrapper over the pair of trousers. Last night it was *Cece Winans*, now *Our Daily Manna*. Philip tried to understand what was going on without asking a direct question:

"Where did you get that?"

"I bought it?"

"Any reason why?"

Zainab laughed in disbelief. "For morning devotion of course. I was hoping you were awake."

"I was actually thinking you would need more rest."

"I slept a lot on the bus. I don't sleep that much anyway"

"I see..."

"Yeah"

The crickets were still awake. Somewhere outside they chirped away during the silence that ensued. Philip and Zainab stared at each other through the darkness. She had that smirk on her face that made a man wonder what she was thinking, whether she was deliberating seducing him. She tapped him on the left shoulder playfully and broke the silence:

"Let's have devotion"

Devotion? So, she was a Christian after all. Now how did that happen? That was one story Philip was eager to hear. He watched her make that swift twist with her body turning towards the living room. The corridor was still dark. The light from the living room carved her silhouette in the darkness. Philip followed, amazed.

"How did you become a Christian?" Philip asked some fifteen minutes later.

She laughed.

"Do you want to hear it now or when you return from work?"

"OK. After work then"

"It's a date"

Both burst out laughing.

More than a Week

"All things are lawful for me, but all things are not helpful. All things are lawful for me, but I will not be brought under the power of any." I Corinthians 6:12

Days passed. Philip was beginning to get a little uneasy while he enjoyed the newfound intimacy. He looked forward to getting home every day, there was someone waiting. He looked forward to waking up, there was someone to pray with. He could relax and have a good home-made meal cooked for him. He could not have Oha or Ukazi or Edikang Ikong but Zainab's Yoruba Egusi soup was Nigerian enough to be enjoyed by an Igbo.

Zainab had not mentioned why she had been there two weeks. Philip thought about raising it a number of times but thought again, not wanting to give the impression he was sending her away. There was enough room in the house, Zainab was useful and he was enjoying intimacy. Intimacy without intercourse of course. There was no way he was going to touch her, it couldn't happen! or couldn't it? Did not having sex really make living with a lady acceptable? Philip had come to think so, it seemed. he was not so bothered about it like he was in the beginning.

Saturday evening. It would have made a nice evening to have a meal out with Abena. He thought about it for a moment while watching a movie on TV. The bubble in the house was a little low this afternoon with Zainab locked away in her room fast alseep. She had sure gotten used to the room, Philip thought. Silence was a great brewing pot for a plethora of thoughts and fantasies; good and evil. "What if she woke up and wanted to just cuddle?" "What if she was really interested in him and that was why she hadn't left the house yet?" "Did she think *he* wanted her too?" "What would happen if he took her out? Would it stir already glowing embers?".

A number of things scared Philip Ezeani about getting involved with a woman. One was the thought of having sex outside of marriage. He had preached against such far too many times to become a victim. He would not be able to forgive himself. He would not be able to drown the screams of his conscience or even cover up a pregnancy if it came to such. He was also scared about marrying someone who would turn out to be an enemy of his spiritual journey. He had become lukewarm, but he definitely still had vision. He could not contemplate any other life outside the Faith. "Was Zainab really a Christian?" he would ask himself over and over. Why had she let herself be put in such a precarious situation, living with a man and acting like his wife asides bedroom duties. The question bounced back at Philip. Then the phone rang.

"Philip my guy..."

It was Hassan. He had been silent a while. Philip was not particularly excited about having his thoughts suddenly broken but it was also a good jolt back to reality. He picked up the remote and lowered the television volume, adjusted himself on the sofa a bit....

"Hi Hassan. How are you?"

37

"I dey o my brother. How my babe?"

"Your babe?"

"Zainab na..."

Philip could feel something resembling a revolt rising inside him when Hassan used the word. The bond was stronger than he had thought, he was beginning to subconsciously think of Zainab as *his own*. He had always had a problem with calling women by pet names and when others did he winced as if he had a secret interest. Consider it a case of not entering and not letting others enter either.

"Oh. She is fine."

"Anyway, she say make I beg you o. She no no how she go fit tell you. The house wey she get dem never complete am so she go need some small one or two weeks join. Abeg no vex..."

"Well, what can I do? She is already here..."

"My brother abeg no vex."

"OK"

"But she tell me say the place dey alright o.... Una dey enjoy you just forget your boy. Abeg if any job show that side let me know o"

"Noted"

"Ehhh... you no wan make I enjoy like you?"

"Ha ha ha ha..."

"You dey laugh. Abeg how I fit get work permit sef? My brother this country hard o. At least make I come do business."

"My company did mine for me. Sincerely I do not know the process."

"But how you come get the job? How you take apply from Nigeria for job wey dey Ghana? Dem don employ all dem people?"

"Na wa o Hassan. It depends on what they are looking for now. Besides the company is a global company. There are subject matter experts for many different fields. They wanted someone who has what I have, and someone referred them to me"

"God dey o. All this English wey you dey speak give me... you just no wan show me di way. No be Africa we dey?"

"Anyway, Hassan, about two years ago, I started praying for a new job. Along the way I felt God's answer was for me to learn a new skill. While trying to find out what was selling I felt God telling me repeatedly to study Adobe's design software. It seemed simple enough and I already was familiar with CorelDraw so after procrastinating for six months I took a six-week weekend course. "

Philip paused. He hesitated, trying to discern Hassan's reaction to the concept of God telling someone how to further his career.

"So?"

"Well... it was not too long after that my direct boss in Lagos got a call from Accra from an old Ghanaian friend who wanted a Graphic Designer with knowledge of Adobe Photoshop and Flash. He wanted a Nigerian! And here I am."

"So, all this enjoyment is because of Photoshop?"

Philip burst out laughing. 'God uses the foolish things of this world to confound the wise'.

"You will not believe how much a telco, or an oil company is willing to pay for a good branding package. Besides, my boss here knows those who make the money for him. He does not pay everyone the same. I am considered an expatriate!"

"God please speak to me o!"

Philip laughed but not too hard this time. He wondered whether it was a good time to talk about the gospel.

"Maybe he is already speaking to you."

"I know. The next thing you will say now is that I should give my life to Christ and everything will be alright"

"Ha ha... not like that. The purpose of the gospel is not to give you a big job. The gospel gives you a new life and the assurance of entering Heaven"

"E be like say you don enter your own heaven sha"

"Hassan this is not Heaven o. It is just a good job."

Suddenly the line cut. Philip did not think he had deliberately cut the line. Was the conviction getting stronger than he had expected? Philip called him back.

"Sorry my brother," Hassan started, "I ran out of credit. So, you were saying..."

"Yes. Basically, when we give our lives to Jesus Christ he does make our lives more meaningful but that is not the point. The more important thing is that we have the assurance of eternal life. The Bible says in I John 5:12-13 'He that hath Christ hath life. He that hath not Christ hath not life. I write to you who believe in the name of the Son of God that you may know that you have eternal life. And this life is in His Son...'"

"Pastor Phil! Ha ha ha. You still dey quote fire. Money never carry am go?"

Philip laughed heartily again. Then he heard movements. Instinctively he looked at the TV just as he realised it must have been Zainab waking up. There was another pause.

"Phil. Thank you so much. I appreciate. I go think am. Abi you know say I be Muslim, but I go think am shaa"

"Great. Keep in touch."

There was such a rush of joy in Philip's soul. He really felt he had made impact. He really felt Hassan had listened to him. It was not the first time he had spoken to Hassan about the Lord, but this seemed special. For some reason Hassan had been on his trail and had seen the outcome of his life over the years and possibly this

41

could be the means by which God was reaching the young man. Maybe he would have yielded by now if he wasn't surrounded by Muslim relatives. Philip stood and stretched. He didn't notice Zainab had walked into the living room. She leaned by the arched entrance that separated the living room from what could have been the dining room. Philip turned.

"Hi" Zainab started.

Her voice was again that soft version. Her smile could very easily be interpreted as suggestive, but it could also be just her own emotions showing up without her knowledge. Her eyes were fixed on him, saying something that Philip could not decipher. She was so difficult to read, and Philip dared not make a move. Her faith was not really clear, the circumstances were not exactly right, he could not contemplate marriage with her. Something was just not right.

A rush of hormones invaded Philip's brain. Sound judgement was clouded momentarily, and a thousand possibilities seemed to well up inside him all at once, but he simply stood there and enjoyed those few seconds.

"Hello..." Philip responded. He dropped the TV remote that he had been stretching with and walked towards her for no apparent reason. He had his own smirk on and his breathing was slightly above regular tempo. He noticed the shine on her face coming from the film of sweat which was reflecting the lights from the low energy incandescent lamps in the living room. She lowered her eyelids. She reached out with her left hand and stroked his left breast, then ran her fingers upwards and then to the back of his neck.

Philip leaned forward and less deliberately put his forearm around her waist and then his left arm over her shoulder and around her neck. Zainab completed the lock with her right hand around his back. Energy rushed through him. She moaned. Five seconds later Zainab pulled back slowly. Soon their bodily contact was merely at the fingers.

"Thanks" Zainab whispered.

"Welcome"

"I really needed a hug"

"OK"

She quickly pulled further away and walked briskly back to her room and shut the door. Philip stood a while, his head a bit clearer now. He started trying to explain to himself what had just happened. He stood akimbo for a few seconds and then decided he wanted to go visit Abena.

Minutes later he passed by her shut door and called out "I will be back!". She was not his wife! He didn't have to tell her where he was going. She did not respond. Behind the doors she sat up on her bed, leaning against an upright pillow, knees curled up to her bare chest, forearms around her sheens, under the blanket, naked!

The drive was a thoughtful one. It was difficult to understand what was happening to him. he could not quite understand how he got to this point. What point? After all, he had not done anything wrong. He merely hugged his guest. But why did he hug her? Does there have to be a reason for everything? The ten-minute drive had been amplified by Saturday evening traffic giving Philip ample time to think. The ease with which it was possible to switch from a spiritual session on the phone to a sudden rush of carnal desire made it easy for him to sympathize with well-known ministers whose sexual scandals he had heard of - both factual and false. A fall was much easier than he had earlier thought when he was protected by the prying eyes of family and friends who knew he was a Christian. The walls of protection had been lifted with his relocation to Accra and the substance of his inner being was being tested. The verse flashed in his mind again.

"You were perfect in your ways from the day that you were created, until iniquity was found in you."

He recalled the description his pastor back in Lagos had given to that word 'iniquity'. A flaw in the person's being. A flaw that manifests as a series of sins when given the opportunity. A flaw that can be hidden for ages until the opportunity is given for a full expression. A flaw that cannot be hidden forever.

Philip made the last left turn into Abena's street and gradually came to a halt in front of a rusty, old red gate left ajar. It never ceased to amaze him how little attention most Ghanaians in middle class neighbourhoods paid to basic security. They definitely were not used to robbery incidents and probably were not prepared for the frequent incidents of burglaries and armed robberies in the few years before and up till then. Some claimed that the crime rate increased in Accra as Nigerians moved into Ghana in their droves looking for business and stable Universities. Nigerians!

After collecting his thoughts, Philip stepped out of the car and shut it carefully, still looking sombre from deep thoughts. he walked through the gate. The main house was an old house, possibly built as far back as the sixties. He glanced at the porch and said hello to three women sitting on plastic chairs chatting pleasantly. he did his best to smile. He walked towards the back of the house. Abena lived in what some would call the Boys' Quarters behind the main building. It was a little more modern having been built much more recently when the landlady wanted to make better use of the land after her husband's death. The cream coloured walls still looked acceptably fresh.

The entire structure was three rooms or better put three apartments since each front door led into an area complete with a living room, bedroom, kitchen and bathroom for each occupant. Philip went around and knocked on the middle room, Abena's.

"Heiiii... my boyfriend that divorced me!" She exclaimed while unlocking the door. She had seen him through the window.

Philip simply laughed. He never responded to gestures from ladies suggesting intimacy even though he did not reject them explicitly either. he actually enjoyed such affection.

"How are you?" Abena continued.

"I am fine, Abena."

"Please come in"

She was all smiles and visibly excited at seeing him. She never hugged him though, hardly even touched him. Philip perceived her

45

as considering him a good friend and he was impressed with her self-control and sense of emotional togetherness. He could hardly see through her, though at some subtle moments like the first time he took her picture, he had noticed what seemed to be intense blushes hidden under a serious look. He was not quite sure what to do with all that. His problem with her was that while she was very moral and sound in her way of life, she never went to church except on invitation or for some special events. On his part he had hardly ever explicitly discussed the gospel with her except for a certain book he had given her to read. She seemed very unconcerned about spiritual things.

Philip walked into the *hall* as the typical Ghanaian would call it and suddenly felt a chill. he looked up towards the source.

"Big girl... you have bought an air conditioner"

"Hahaha... instalment payment o. Someone came around the office selling electronics on hire purchase and I took advantage"

"I see. Good for you." Philip sank into a chair and Abena on another. His nose came alive at the aroma of jollof rice, but he did not comment on it.

"So, who has been keeping you away from me? Your new guest?"

"Oh. Abena. Naaa... "

Philip's nose could have grown longer at that moment. It was obvious Zainab had his exclusive attention for the past two weeks except when he ran into Helen at the office.

"How is work?"

"Great. Yours?"

"Well... hmmm... it is there o. Boring but what can we do? If you see any opportunities for me, please tell me ooo."

"All that money you are making, and you want to move..."

"it is not just about money, Philip. Do you know how long I have been a teller? Four years... I need a change. Even if it is within the bank"

Philip always admired Abena's sense of direction in life. She had done so well for herself. Her independence was inspiring. She had learnt to take care of herself quite early. Her parents had passed, and she was an only child, raised by Uncles and Aunts and Grandmas. That must be where she got all that emotional strength. He also loved the fact that he could sit with her for hours alone and not be erotically aroused. The friendship seemed so pure.

"Hope you will have some jollof?" Abena asked.

"Of course. What bachelor would refuse a good meal?"

They laughed. It was so easy to make Abena laugh, so natural. Eating together had become normal for them over the previous few months even on Saturday Mornings when Philip finished from a certain early morning prayer meeting near her place.

"It smells good" Philip continued. They exchanged smiles for a few seconds before Abena turned her attention to the TV. She always

47

watched the evening news and was up to date, another attraction for Philip.

"Have you heard, they are going to build an interchange at Kwame Nkrumah Circle o"

"Oh yeah... I overheard it at the office."

"It will make things so much easier. At least I wouldn't have to wake up so early and pass the long route through Kokomlemle..."

"Yeah. I am sure by the time it is done like fifteen minutes will get you to North Ridge"

"In fact. It is a good move, but I learnt the government borrowed the money o"

"Really? From who?"

"Who else? IMF. With all their unbearable conditions..."

"Well as long as the money is used to do what they borrowed it for. back in Nigeria, like three quarters of it would be going to Switzerland!"

"Switzerland?"

Abena stared at Philip. Anything that sounded like new knowledge always caught her attention.

"Yes. Most corrupt government officials in Nigeria are known to stack stolen money away in Swiss bank accounts."

"And the whites don't say anything?"

"What are they going to say? You work in a bank. Do you ask your customers how they got their money before accepting deposits?"

"Oh no Philip but it's not the same!"

Philip just laughed. Abena sprang up. "Lemme check the rice". Philip followed her with his eyes. She was fascinating. An intellectually stimulating discussion with an intelligent lady always made a strong impression on him. He could talk on and on with Abena and it seemed there were few women like her in his life possibly because he never went looking for them, they either came to him, ran into him or were introduced to him. He set his eyes back on the TV and partially listened as Abena talked about her cooking"

"As if I knew you were coming... I would not have been able to finish this food"

"How different is Nigerian rice to Ghanaian rice?"

"I can imagine when last you ate a great meal like this... hahaha"

She never seemed to run out of things to say but she was not irksome, it was fun listening to her. She seemed always in control, no emotional expressions were in excess.

Dinner was served, and they ate together like brother and sister amidst laughter and friendly disputes on current affairs and ideologies. Soon more than two hours had passed but it seemed like a few minutes. Philip asked to take his leave and Abena agreed without hesitation. It was so difficult to tell whether she wanted him to stay a little longer. Philip just could not tell. On the way out, they said hello to the lone woman at the veranda on the main house. Abena said hello and just carried on seeing Philip off while he himself wondered what the woman would think about a man coming out of her house at that time of the night. He always wondered what people would think. On occasion he pondered within himself whether his restraint on certain actions was motivated by people's opinions or actually God's expectations.

In another twenty minutes Philip was at his gate. He let himself in as usual and just as he opened the main door he noticed Zainab's silhouette on the couch in the living room. He was a bit surprised she was still awake.

"Where have you been?" She asked in a certain tone.

"What?" Philip almost whispered. It was totally unexpected. Why would she ask him that? Something had gone amiss. What were her expectations? What right did she have to ask him about his movements? Surely this was not an issue of accountability, this was an intrusion! She was here as a guest and for all intents and purposes she had overstayed .... Why would she have the boldness to ask his whereabouts?

Philip was silent for a few seconds articulating the appropriate answer then she seemed to come to herself:

"I mean at least if you leave the house you should at least tell someone you left at home that you would be home late! It's almost eleven! I know it's your house but if something happens to you while I am here, I will be asked! Good night."

He watched her calmly stand up and walk to her room. A smile grew on his face. This was totally unexpected, but she was right in a way. Philip had somehow become used to the single life and was beginning to forget how to live with someone, especially a woman. But, this was definitely an intrusion. Intimacy brewing and becoming like a huge tree in the centre of his life. Disturbing.

Intimacy is an intrusion into your lonely lifestyle, a bold invasion of your privacy often with your consent. It just happens to be a very pleasant invasion ... most of the time. Intimacy happens when you cross paths with another species of being and find that your numerous plugs fit into their numerous sockets... at least most of them. Intimacy happens when you open up your sockets and extend your plugs to exchange soul by giving and receiving.

Intimacy is an invasion. There are no more gates with this significant other. There are no more barriers. There is so much discomfort in tearing down these barriers and when they are down... they are down. The army raids your inward parts, and nothing is hidden anymore. Whatever was in the dark is completely exposed. The fragile emotions, the unseemly habits, the lousy flaws covered in cosmetics in public places. Everything is exposed!

Intimacy is an intrusion. At the beginning, it is unpleasant to give in. But when the bombardment becomes unbearable, the walls begin to fall. They crack at first, it hurts yet is thrilling. Why does the thrill hurt so much? Because stone

51

walls are crumbling under heavy fire. The women of the city are on rampage. There is chaos in the inward parts. The boundaries are no longer relevant.

Intimacy is an invasion. Looting is lawful because everything is shared. Nothing is private anymore when two become one. The concept of private property has no meaning in this realm. The other one becomes a disturbance that you cannot live without, a massive cedar tree growing in the centre of your bedroom. Things get missing, personal effects are moved, and permissions are granted without being requested. Everything is shared.

Intimacy is liberation when two become one; that is how we are designed. Intimacy is a relief because that is what we long for. Intimacy is a pedestal which we all reach for so long as we have the capacity to feel. Intimacy is a challenge we find fulfilling to surmount. Intimacy is a trap we would gladly walk into over and over again because we would rather be bound by love than be lost in loneliness.

Intimacy is a seed that can grow for a lifetime. Intimacy is a weed that can become beautiful when nurtured or else entangled to the point of choking itself when left untended. Intimacy is an experience so sacred and priceless, so profound and engaging, so complex and intricate that it can only be shared with one other at any point in time during a lifetime.

Intimacy is a treasure often so hard to find and so easy to lose that we must depend on neither logic nor appearance to grasp its deepest meaning. A concept so deep that we must spend a lifetime discovering its infinite layers and facets. It is a maze so intricate that we must pay attention to the tiniest detail to preserve it in its finest form. Intimacy . . . we could go on and on forever and we will.

Kenneth Igiri, July 2012

Boundary Lines

"Therefore, let him who thinks he stands take heed lest he fall." 1 Corinthians 10:12

"Hi Philip" the tinge of excitement in Zainab's voice was suspicious. What was she up to this time? He was just rounding up a project when her call came in. He became used to being called at close of work to buy something along the way or come early or something else. He was not so comfortable with this intrusion, but he never complained. At least not to her.

"Zainab. Howdy," Philip sounded more like he could have said 'What is it now?'. His tone did not deter Zainab. Her excitement remained intact.

"Please buy popcorn when coming home, OK"

"OK"

Philip did not bother asking why but she answered anyway "I got the latest Fringe series!"

"OK"

The calls were often that short. Philip was simply not comfortable with her acting as if she was his wife. It was getting more and more serious.

54

"Hmmm... who was that, Philip. Who has taken my *husby* away?"

It was Helen. She had been at the door to his cubicle for a few seconds. The blush on his face gave him away, she knew it must have been a woman. She helped herself to a chair and sat facing Philip.

"So, when are you leaving?" she asked looking him straight in the face.

"Soon". Philip fiddled with his mouse. The internal pressure was mounting. Zainab, Helen .. Abena.... He kept his eyes on his display, wishing Helen would go away but she would not. She was not one to back out in a fight. She did perceive this as a fight, someone seemed to be getting Philip's attention. How could she have known that that someone had a much better chance if it all came down to a struggle for the young man: she lived with him!

"So, would you be interested in Pizza?"

"Pizza?"

"Yup"

Philip chuckled. Having a woman chase him always felt so thrilling. He considered being asked out a 'chase'. It could just be a case of the woman giving him a chance to chase them since he seemed so lethargic about the whole matter. Some women were serious enough about their lives to try to find out whether a friendship with him was going anywhere. They were honest enough to accept that they liked him and wanted to see if he liked them too. He just enjoyed the thrill but had not made up his mind about anyone in particular.

"I could get to know your place afterwards..."

"My place?" Philip looked up at her. All sorts of alarms went off in his head! Most of them started with the letter "Z". He certainly could not allow another woman visit him under his present circumstances even though he would certainly have loved to have Helen come around. Abena would have been OK but Helen? No! Abena was less attached in his estimation and he had already told her about Zainab. How would he explain to Helen what Zainab was doing in his house? And maybe this was how marriage would be after all these adventures in singleness: you have to live with just one woman and all others would be at a distance! Why did this seem such a difficult way to live for Philip? Something must have been amiss in his soul.

It seemed to be the Gentle Voice again referring to a verse from the Inspired Writings "from all appearance of evil, abstain ye;". Certainly, there was something uncanny about Zainab's presence in his house that made him uncomfortable about letting people know, especially since most people who knew him knew he was a Christians of the "Born Again" class.

"What's wrong? You don't want me to know your place?"

"Not that..."

"Then what? It's just a friendly visit... I am not going to rape you! So what about Pizza?"

"Err..."

"In fact, just forget I asked..."

Helen rose and left. She glanced at him one more time just as she packed her handbag and left the office. Philip could have sworn he felt physical pain from that look on her face. He certainly would not drink anything she offered him anytime soon. He knew she was interested in him, but the encounter today was scary. Was it his fault? Had he been 'leading her on' as they say? He could not really tell. She did not speak to him for a week, just glances.

Who would have known she felt so strongly about him? He didn't. Or at least he thought he could easily shake her off. On her part it was a wakeup call. The thought of another woman getting his attention was something she did not expect in such a short time. She did not quite know how to deal with it. She had no claim on him, but she could not let go easily either.

Popcorn was served later that evening, in front of Philip's large TV screen. Fringe was a Sci-Fi series about a certain mad scientist who had discovered an alternate universe where there was a copy of everyone in this universe. Some film makers were certainly on the fringes over in Hollywood - the boundary between insanity and reality.

Zainab was in her shorts again but partly covered up her legs with a wrapper. She loved freedom. Both sat on the floor, the rug was so soft and warm, it was easy to manoeuvre on. Philip sat further away from the television and could see a glimmer on her face most likely from a little sweat, the kind that came on a lady's face when she wanted a man badly. There was a part of Philip that felt he was doing a lady a favour when he responded to her emotional need. That part had not yet fully understood love and commitment; the real desire in a woman's heart - a long term relationship.

Zainab suddenly sprang up, paused the TV and walked briskly to her room.

"I'll be back. " she mumbled.

"OK"

The atmosphere was tense again as it had been for more than a few nights since she was in the house. Something seemed to change the emotional climate dramatically between 6:00 PM and 10:00 PM. It became worse if they stayed up late. Zainab came back in a minute with her violin. She sat on the couch, laid the instrument gently on her left shoulder and began playing a tune. She was very relaxed in her seat, legs apart; again in her jeans shorts. She had left her wrapper in the room as she picked the violin. It took seconds for Philip the recognise the tune she was playing: Celine Dion's *My Heart Will Go On.* It was very popular in his school days and he did remember some of the words clearly as the theme song for the movie *Titanic.* He never failed to feel a little dirty when he enjoyed secular songs. It was one of the first things he learnt to nail to the cross when he became a Christian. it was an interesting point of debate among contemporary Christians: "should we listen to secular songs or not?" "What is actually wrong with love songs?" "Can I dance to love songs with my wife?" and on and on.

Philip found Zainab's skill at the violin impressive. Where had she learnt to play like that. He listened for a few more minutes and stopped abruptly in the middle of the song. She then started playing Michael Smith's *Breathe*. She played the entire song in about ten minutes. All that time Philip simply listened quietly, his attention swaying back and forth between the movie and Zainab. He could not fight the attraction. So many things about Zainab called out to him: her sassiness, her talkativeness, her height, her wit, her culinary skills and now her musical prowess. She could be a lot of fun to live with but for the fact that he wasn't quite sure of her spiritual convictions. His were strong though he had managed to break a lot of rules.

"So..." began Zainab.

"... what do you think?"

"About?". Philip thought it might be nice to play along.

"The songs"

Zainab slipped deliberately and sat on the floor again with her back against the couch. She dropped the violin on the couch and spread out her arms tapping the couch with her fingers. Her legs were still apart. She made a bridge with her right knee and lay the left on the floor. Philip thought about telling her to go and get her wrapper but hesitated. He always tried not to seem offensive or judgemental even at his own peril. it was the *phleg* in him: get along with everyone.

"Well. You play well"

Zainab laughed hard.

"Is that all? Why can't you just pass a simple compliment?"

A quick *deja vu* flashed on Philip's consciousness: A colleague once told him he was sorry for his wife because he seemed to be bereft of the skills required to stir a woman with words. He considered it keeping his emotions to himself, avoiding stirring up emotions. he even had a scripture for it:

"I charge you, O daughters of Jerusalem, by the gazelles, and by the does of the field, do not stir up or awake my Love until He please."
Songs of Solomon 2:7

Zainab raised her bridged left leg towards herself and drew back her left arm and dropping it carelessly on her left thigh, caressing a little. With her elbow on the couch, she made a fist and rested her chin on it, staring straight at Philip.

"Say after me, 'Zainab, I love the way you play the violin'". She laid emphasis on the third word. Philip blushed, and she noticed even in the partial darkness. She roared with laughter flinging her left arm back on the couch.

What was Zainab's intention. She has a Muslim name but reads the Bible and claims to be saved. She consistently prompts him for Bible study and prayer yet puts up this strongly flirtatious behaviour every now and then. Was she a believer or not? Was she some agent of Satan sent to pull him down? Or was he himself down already? She moved closer and sat beside him on the floor resting her head on his shoulder. he did not react. "So, do you like

Celine Dion?". Philip just chuckled. There was silence for a few minutes. Zainab sat up and started playing again. The Fringe series video had switch to the next episode and caught Philip's attention. He glanced at the TV and turned his attention back to Zainab's solo orchestra. She stopped suddenly.

"You are enjoying it, aren't you?"

Philip did not respond.

"Why are you torturing yourself? Why don't you just be yourself? So, have you sinned now that you listened to this nice song? It's a song! There is nothing wrong with it!"

"Is there anything *right* with it? Why is it so important that I should enjoy it?"

Zainab let out another round of hysterical laughter.

"I am not asking you to start enjoying it. I know you're already enjoying and you are trying to resist. That's all. I want you to be free..."

With that she left her violin on the floor and leaned on him again, this time she was more relaxed, she stared at her bridged knee, undulating like a pendulum with her butt as the fulcrum. She had tucked her head under Philip's chin and her hair tickled him.

"Free from what?"

"Free to express yourself my dear! Christianity is not bondage"

The words of Paul, the Apostle lit up Philip's mind:

"No, I keep on disciplining my body, making it serve me so that after I have preached to others, I myself will not somehow be disqualified."

Malcom X in his time spoke of the divergent views *Home Slaves* and *Field Slaves* had of their bondage. "Back during slavery," Malcolm begins, "there were two kinds of slaves. There was the house Negro and the field Negro. The house Negroes — they lived in the house with master, they dressed pretty good, they ate good 'cause they ate his food — what he left. They lived in the attic or the basement, but still they lived near the master; and they loved their master more than the master loved himself. They would give their life to save the master's house quicker than the master would ... Whenever the master said 'we,' he said 'we.' That's how you can tell a house Negro."

...

"And if you came to the house Negro and said, 'Let's run away, let's escape, let's separate,' the house Negro would look at you and say, 'Man, you crazy. What you mean, separate? Where is there a better house than this? Where can I wear better clothes than this? Where can I eat better food than this?' That was that house Negro. In those days he was called a 'house nigger.' And that's what we call him today, because we've still got some house niggers running around here."

Slavery is experienced in a variety of ways. Some people enjoy their slavery, but it doesn't change their status. *Freedom* can be interpreted in a number of ways. Freedom can be considered being released from controlling factors - slave masters, habits, drugs, and even our own emotions and human tendencies. Another view of freedom is being released from any kind of restraint. Zainab was referring to the latter kind of freedom. She wanted Philip to let go of himself, dispose of all restraints and just do whatever he felt like doing. Freedom. Paul spoke of freedom as overcoming his natural inclinations and making his body the slave rather than himself. Zainab considered freedom as allowing the body to rule. One was definitely easier than the other that is why it felt more like freedom. Freedom that comes from surrendering rather than fighting. Is one really free if one does not fight for his freedom? Or has one simply surrendered?

Philip continued, "God created an order in the Universe. We cannot just act the way we want in the name of freedom. Someone can want something and still know within themselves that what they want is the wrong thing!"

"*Oyibo*!"

"See. Think about a child..."

Zainab sat up and faced him, leaning forward and supporting herself with her left arm. Her sheens now lay on the floor and the sole of her foot face upwards, her toes pointing backwards away from Philip. There was just about a foot and half between them. Philip could hear her breath and could almost feel it.

"I'm listening"

"... if you were a mother frying some plantain, would you give a piece straight from the oil to your little girl just because she asked?"

"Of course!"

"What?"

"When she experiences the heat, she will drop it and learn a lesson!"

"Oh Zainab!"

"Some people have not even experienced anything, and they claim it is bad, it is a sin, it is this it is that... how do you know?"

She stuck her face in his momentarily when she let out the last phrase seemingly challenging him. He was lost.

"What are you talking about?"

"Celine Dion," Zainab snapped, laughing out loud. If Philip did not know better, he would have thought she was drunk. Something was definitely making her a little tipsy. Zainab sprang up and again. She seemed to be going to the *washroom* but did not say. Philip had some time to evaluate the situation. It had been more than a month and things were getting a little out of hand. He did not know whether to tell her to leave by all means or make a new set of rules about boundaries or call Hassan's attention. It was just all very confusing. He knew what needed to be done but had no power to do it. Where would she go? And why hadn't Hassan called in weeks anyway? Philip had to call him and talk. It was obvious to him that

64

Zainab wanted something more than an innocent stay in the house of a friend's friend, but should he confront her with that directly? He had towed that line with ladies in the past and found it not very pleasant especially with Christian woman. he ended up looking like the one with a depraved mind. 'Renew your mind' they would say, 'Why are you thinking like that?', 'Are we not brother and sister?'. People lie or attempt to lie to others, but the naked truth hunt them in their souls. Some things can be explained as being OK, but they would still not really feel OK. Zainab living with Philip simply did not feel OK.

Zainab ran into the living room and slid in between his legs startling him out of his thoughts. She sat with her back leaning on his chest. Her loose hair rubbed against his left cheek.

"Did I tell about the time I went to visit a friend in Abuja only to find out she had travelled?"

"Nope"

"When I was serving in Kwara State. Can you imagine what she told me when I called her?"

"Tell me"

"She asked me to call her boyfriend to pick me up!"

"I see"

Bells always went off in Philip's head when certain words were mentioned in conversation. *boyfriend, girlfriend, love, sex* etc. His definitions of some of the terms were more often than not quite different from the traditional 21st century definitions.

"He took me to his place..."

Philip was now beginning to wonder the purpose of the story.

"I stayed at his place till Sunday evening when my friend came back. And it was just one room with two other boys. And it was fun!"

Zainab giggled.

"I see"

"What do you see?"

"What response were you expecting?"

She giggled again.

"I don't know..." she continued, "I took them like my brothers. We slept together on the same mattress on the floor."

"All four of you?"

"Some people move about a lot when they sleep. Deji kept rolling off the bed! ha ha"

"I see"

"Do you have sisters?"

"Yes..."

"How do you relate with them?"

"Cordially. At least I don't cuddle with them"

Zainab laughed so much she stretched out, ecstatic. She was unbelievably at ease resting her entire weight on Philip. he did not seem to object and she kept going further and further. He had not said stop so she guessed everything was OK so far. She started speaking with that soft version of her voice:

"Philip..."

She hardly called his name directly. He answered, and she paused for a moment.

"Are you a virgin?"

Flashback. A few years before he had answered the same question on the phone with a strange lady he had called. He had picked up the number from page three of a popular soft sell. Her name was Vivian. On the phone he had found out she was a member of The Redemption Centre, a very well-known church in Lagos. She was on the Audio/Visual team in church and that made him wonder what she was doing on page three. She had laughed hysterically when he told her he was a virgin at almost thirty. Why would a *Born Again Christian* lady find it funny that a single person is a virgin? Well why would a Born Again Christian man be calling a page three girl whom he did not know from Adam? Questions arising....

"Well, as it is, I am not sure?"

67

"Not sure. Philip have you had sex or not?"

He was surprised she didn't laugh at that one.

"Not exactly"

"Philip!"

He laughed a little himself.

"Well it is not a laughing matter though. I was kind of used when I was about seven. Our house help made me do things I did not understand. Losing my 'virginity' was part of those things. But I am not sure I even had a virginity at seven. What do you think?"

"Seriously?" a smile broke out on her face, temporarily suspending her own emotionally troubling memories, "Did you enjoy it?"

"I am not sure... I think it has even made me recoil at the thought of intercourse. Even in marriage."

Zainab was beginning to think he deliberately avoided the word *sex*.

"Would you like to experience it again?"

"I am not enthusiastic, actually. What about you?"

"Whether I am enthusiastic about sex?"

"Are you a virgin?"

"Almost!"

"I see"

She laughed.

"I am answering like you now." she started, "I was a virgin till I was twenty-four. I always resisted men. All through university I did not sleep with anyone. Even when I was serving many men wanted me both on and off campus. I wanted to give my husband a good gift, so I resisted..."

She spoke as though she really regretted something that had happened in her past. Philip listened, feeling for her yet a little suspicious. Emotional engagement is a well-known method of trapping people in a variety of scenarios. Social Engineering is based on engaging people emotionally. People have been duped based on pity. In fact, up till then, even Philip's thinking had been muddied because his hormones were working harder than his cerebrum. How else could one explain the personal details he had let out to Zainab, things he had not told even very close family members. She was merely drawing him deeper into this river into which he had already stepped?

She continued, "... until I met him. I told him over and over again I didn't want sex but he took advantage of me in my moment of weakness. I only needed a shoulder to lean on and he took advantage of me. I told him to stop and he would not listen..."

Philip became curious about who this "him" was but felt it wasn't such a good idea to ask right then. He thought he heard her sob. His hands both found their way on top of her belly. He pulled her in closer to himself.

69

"*Broda* Philip," she mocked, giggling. Philip made a hesitant move to withdraw but her forearm was now over his, holding them down softly.

The Reason Why

"What do you mean when you use this proverb concerning the land of Israel, saying: 'The fathers have eaten sour grapes, And the children's teeth are set on edge'?" Ezekiel 18:2

Distant relationships were good for Philip's non-committal disposition. It was easier to flirt on Facebook or over the phone than sit with a lady at a bar. It seemed safer, less "sinful" if you wish. No touching, no *lookery*, just talk. Many young ladies from Philip's day in Nigeria were willing to chat with him for hours. Why wouldn't they be willing to try their luck with a successful, accomplished young man living "abroad". Besides he was born again so that should mean it was safe and maybe he would finally propose. He didn't take many of them very seriously, he wasn't really concerned about commitment but simply enjoyed company. He did have a few committed friends, some with whom there were possibilities, others out of reach. Emem, Patricia, Amarachi (Mrs.) and Lara were the top five on the list of women he would call great friends.

He had met Emem only once physically as a possible candidate during a brief visit to New Haven, Enugu. They were both part of a Blackberry Group created for the purpose of helping couples and intending couple thrive. Philip was smuggled in so everyone was looking for a wife in the group for him. Emem was the most talkative young lady Philip had ever met but almost everything she said made a lot of sense. She was extra intelligent though she talks unstoppably when she became engaged. The profuseness of her words did not mar their quality and Philip enjoyed just listening to her on the phone. When they finally met in Enugu months before he moved to Accra, the meeting was so full of blushes that Emem hardly spoke. he was attracted to her and so was she. His perfectionist tendencies hindered his move. he watched her and examined every detail of her body, outfit, expressions, hairdo.... He could have drawn a picture of her after that meeting. She was tall, at least five feet six, a slim size 8 and had high shoulders. The few spots on her face did not mar her skin too badly. He spent four hours with her that evening, but it did not result in a relationship, at least not anything leading to marriage. After that meeting they spoke on the phone or chatted on BBM every day for two weeks non-stop until Philip freaked out. He slowed things down. he was impressed at her response. She did not withdraw or feel wounded like some, she just reduced the frequency of her calls and chatted more. he did more of the calling when he moved.

Patricia was a sister he knew from a young people's fellowship he had led before he went to the university. They had a thing going but it was not romantic. She wasn't physically attractive to him but her personality was rare. She laughed a whole lot, had spiritual depth and simply just knew him well. She offers to do amazing things for him with no strings attached. By some stroke of chance or providence, they ended up in the same University two years apart. She would cook meals for him and bring to his room, run errands when he was working on his final year project, get him things from home when she travelled. It was amazing. The relationship spilled over to real life and they met in Lagos and kept talking. She hardly called but when she did it was a long chat like old friends meeting again. She even planned holidaying in Accra, but he dissuaded her. He knew he would have to be the one to take care of her and somehow wanted to avoid that.

Mrs. Amarachi Ade-Williams could have been Mrs. Amarachi Ezeani almost a decade previously. He loved her from their first year, but they finally got close working together in their third-year project. Maybe Philip had not tried hard enough. Maybe he was too spiritual about his approach. maybe he did not look like someone ready for marriage back in his final year when he proposed marriage to her the first time. She was the only woman he had tried such a venture with. He could not take the response, it did not turn out positive. It was compounded by two other "NOs" the year after and the year after the year after. the amazing thing was they were always very good friends and he interpreted her concern for love. She had already set her wedding date when he made the last attempt and someone else had to tell him she was engaged already.

How could he have known. She knew he loved her too much and did not know how to communicate the true situation of things softly. It had to come from a mutual friend of theirs. She was herself interested in Philip to a fault and was glad to tell him that Amara was gone so maybe he could then open his eyes and see her. He didn't. Well he did open his eyes but he didn't see her.

Lara was a true friend. Back then they lived in the same neigbourhood and were always at each other's throats. Everyone thought they made a good match since they could quarrel so much and still remain friends. She had moved to South Africa and then to Seychelles, earning a lot of money but still single. She was herself very choosy and he knew just about every man who had tried to woo her as well as their list of flaws. She knew his stories too, including the details about Mrs. Ade-Williams. She never thought of him as a prospect. They grew up together, like brother and sister. It was weird but true, long term relationships seemed to fail translation to marriage. or maybe they just took each other for granted and kept looking elsewhere for something or someone more exciting. the exciting always become the normal.

Mrs. Ade-Williams was on Philip's mind after being married for five years. They spoke every now and then. She was pleasant, courteous and tried to emphasize to him that it was impossible for him to be married to her. She was married. She did not say this directly, she just told him stories of men who really liked her and how she responded to them nicely but firmly. her husband was almost out of the country and when she did not go with him, she was out and about in Abuja or elsewhere with her kids or alone. She haunted him. Why hadn't it worked out? Why was he the second best on her list. A list of reason would flood his mind every now and then. He could have had two or three kids. It was most likely because he did not have a good job then. Money. That was it! Money.

Philip was always put off by rich, blue chip company alumni coming back to school to marry young ladies. he always concluded money had something to do with the equation. Old? Well, to someone in his early twenties, thirty-five was old especially when the bride in question happened to be one of his playmates. Someone had mentioned to him back then that financial security was an inescapable aspect of the marriage contract. Well they

74

hadn't used those words, they didn't have such sophisticated, poetic vocabulary back then.

That evening, he would call her to settle the issue. Why did she reject him? It was a bother for years. He got back to his empty house early. Mr. Anani, his neighbour had come out to check who it was. He normally wasn't home this early. While unlocking the door he stared into his iPhone. He had ignored two more calls from Victoria that day. Contacts. Search. Amarachi Onuoma. Yes, he still stored her number with her maiden name. Such severe hurts were hidden deep in his subconscious.

"My big brother in Accra! Been a while." Philip heard after a ring or two.

Amarachi often answered the phone in an excited tone with expressions that he interpreted as affection somewhere in his subconscious. Little did he know that she was just as excited about every one of her close male or female friends. This affection detection was just something he made up in his own mind; his own love for her bouncing off and hitting him. These mind games we play on ourselves....

Philip chuckled. Amarachi continued.

"What is tickling you? Anyway, how are you doing and to what do we owe the honour of this august call?"

"Ha Ha. Well I just thought to say hello..."

"OK. Good idea. It's been long since we heard from you?"

"Well, sometimes I just like to keep my distance for a while to avoid being too intrusive?"

Amarachi burst out laughing. Philip blushed, embarrassed that he had said things that made little or no sense.

"Intruding in what? Na you sabi! Philip na wa for you o. Renew your mind, we are just friends as long as you are OK with that."

"Of course, you are still my friend, but I often feel I am intruding..."

"*I hu kwa! O zu go, biko*"

Philip laughed out loud again. He had always admired Amarachi's bluntness. It was one of her most significant advantages with him. She could never hold anything she needed to say back.

"So how may I help you? Before you tell me, my time is up since you are now regulating your friends ..." Amarachi added. Philip chuckled again.

He felt so at home with her. They could talk for hours none stop. But she was now another man's and he needed to respect that. He had been absolutely convinced she was for him back in the day. In his final year he had had so many dreams about her which he interpreted as messages from God that he could not convince himself he was wrong even if he tried. He had even told David Osiezaga, a fellowship leader and a close mutual friend that if it did not turn out that she married him, he would conclude that God does not speak through dreams! Dreams. Such tricky experiences.

Philip's mind roamed and arrived at events six to eight years earlier. On a certain occasion he had returned to school to sort out issues regarding his National Service. He arrived Friday morning and planned to leave the same weekend. He had been communicating with her for a couple of months: emails, phone calls, Yahoo Chat. Love notes, poems, reports of his life's progress. Things seemed OK.

"Philip. Are you there?" she broke into his thoughts sharply. He must have been lost in the past for ten seconds.

"Yeah. Yeah. Errr..."

"So, have you finally chosen someone?"

He didn't laugh this time. His mood had been dampened by memories.

"No. Not yet..."

"Oh Philip. when?"

"I actually wanted to ask something..."

"I see. More important than your getting married?"

"Well... I guess it is in fact about my marriage?"

"I see. Shoot..."

"I don't want you to be taken aback by this. I just need to know, and I think it is time for me to really know..."

"I am listening"

Amarachi herself was now a little suspicious. What was this about?

"I would like to know why we did not get married"

There was a pause of five seconds. It seemed like the half-life of a carbon fourteen isotope. At least to Philip. Had he asked the unthinkable. He had hurriedly blurted it all out not allowing himself the luxury of a change of mind after the prolonged small talk. Philip waited. Carbon isotope. Breathing on both sides was heavy for those seconds. Amarachi answered very deliberately. He noticed the change in her tone.

"Philip. I actually thought we had gone past this? Why are you asking me this after close to seven years? You are living in the past, Philip! You need to let go. Oh! Unbelievable..."

Philip waited.

"Philip look, the answer to this question is of zero use to you right now. As in zero!'

"I still want to know"

"I am changing the topic"

"Amara, why is it a problem to answer this question"

"Why are you just asking the question, Sir?"

Amarachi wanted to end the call so badly but the strength of the relationship did not let her go that far. She was upset to say the least. In her mind everything about a possible romantic relationship was over with years ago. They were friends, just great friends. The tension on this call was unhealthy. Amarachi did not see this coming. Philip was not backing down; he had to have the answer. The call ended.

What? She ended the call. That was a big shock to Philip. How could she do that? He redialed the number and got feedback from his telephone company's recording: he had run out of airtime. Unbelievable how expensive it had become to call Nigeria. Amarachi was grateful for the break.

"He cut the call on me" she blurted out and turned from the dining table to her husband. He chuckled.

"You and your boyfriend are quarrelling"

As far as Amarachi was concerned, Dapo was the most easy-going man she had met. She, taking into account her happy-go-lucky nature, could not have imagined a more accommodating husband. Oladapo was it!

"Oh, Dapo this is serious! How can he be asking me why we didn't get married?"

Oladapo Ade-Williams dropped the book in his hand face down on his lap. Part of the book was on his shorts and the other on his naked right thigh. He felt the cold from the paper.

"So why don't you want to tell him?"

"Why should I? It doesn't make sense. What has he been thinking all these years? You men are funny o"

Dapo Chuckled again. He had such a calm disposition like someone completely consumed by the Holy Spirit. Never upset, never disturbed, never worried. Life was very simple for him and this made him a great match for Amarachi.

"So, what will you lose by telling him? Maybe it will help. "

Amarachi gave her husband a queer look.

"You don't want to hurt him. Well maybe he is already hurt and has been hurt for a long time. You know Philip is a very deep person, he must have taken his time before deciding to propose to you so maybe he has not forgotten you like you think he has. Some people handle such things much more easily than others..."

"Look Dapo I just do not understand it. Why will he not just forget me and marry someone else? It bothers me! When he called I even thought he was going to tell me he had someone now. He is acting immature *abeg*!"

Another chuckle.

The phone rang again. She did not pick. She was not ready to continue the discussion. Philip was not giving up on this either. It had hunted him for far too long and he had to end it. What would he do with the answer? Nothing was going to change; his first love was married to someone else. It was a struggle for him back then, watching those who had graduated long before him living in big cities all over the world return to campus years after graduation to woo sisters whom he considered his playmates. School does that to one, obscures some of the realities of life. He wouldn't have imagined that someday he himself would repeat the same cycle.

Philip called again. She picked this time. She could not keep ignoring him, she cared too much. Another difficulty Philip had: distinguishing among the numerous complex emotional expressions of woman with similar symptoms. In his dealings with the many women in his life, he often found himself asking bizarre questions: Does she love me or just care about me? Does she pity me or like me? Does she think of me as a possible candidate or just as a nice brother? Does she have feelings for me specifically or is she just being as nice to me as she is to everyone else? Complications! Part of the problem was that he often asked only one person these questions: himself.

"Hello," Amarachi answered, doing her best to strip her voice of all emotion.

"Amara"

"Yes...". She smiled to herself, enjoying the pursuit in some way. She always wanted him to be more aggressive. Maybe that was the catch? Aggression. Philip lacked aggression. He would rather wait for a lady to come to him. And they just kept coming.

"Amara, I need to know. I would not have called you at this hour if I did not really want an answer"

"So, you want an answer?"

"Yes, please"

81

"Are you ready for any answer?"

"Yes?"

"In fact, what are you even going to do with this answer?"

"Amara!"

"Look Philip do not raise your voice at me. That is uncalled for. You are trying to dig up something that is dead and buried. I am sorry but that is what I said: dead and buried! You have to move on. Move on, Philip!"

"I am sorry for raising my voice, but you are stretching me. Just tell me what I need to know. I do not intend to disturb you. There is no need to drag this. Just tell me where I went wrong. Maybe it would help me understand myself better."

Amara thought for a while and then calmed down for a minute. She knew she needed to communicate the truth gently even though she felt it was totally unnecessary. Philip was digging up dry bones.

"Philip," She started, "First I want you to know that I have always respected you and considered you a great person. As a person, you are great. There is no doubt about that. I hope you know that that is my opinion of you?"

"I appreciate that"

"So, there is nothing wrong with you per se. I simply had to make a choice that I felt was in line with God's will for my life. Aside this, I sought counsel and arrived at the fact that two people from broken homes may have a tough time balancing their roles as husband and wife. Nothing more. I considered that wise counsel and made my choice based on God's leading. Now I really want us to leave this matter behind and look ahead. Believe me I have been praying for you to find the right person for you and I believe we can still contribute to each other's lives positively. *O kwa ya*[3]?"

Philip was so silent and the atmosphere so tense that Amarachi wondered whether she had done the right thing. She called out to him twice and received no answer. She called a third time:

"Philip, are you there?"

"But..." Philip's voice shook. She was afraid he would shed tears. he definitely had not seen that coming. The implications were profound. His naivety became even more apparent to him. How could he have assumed so much?

Amarachi made facial expressions to her husband showing her discomfort at the awkward situation. She could have given anything to drop the call at that moment but that would have complicated the issue. she fidgeted on her seat by the dining table, uncomfortable.

"Philip, you said you were ready for the answer. That is the answer o. I hope we are still friends?"

---

[3] Igbo for "Isn't it so?"

He could almost feel the smile on her face at the other end of the telephone line. The genuineness of her love and patience was simply hard to find. He breathed deeply.

"OK. Thanks Amara. I completely understand. I appreciate your telling me this and I am willing to be friends."

He did his best to sound in control even though the answer weighed heavily on him. It was not what he expected. But what did he expect? He wasn't quite sure. One part of him was satisfied that he had received an answer, another part was not satisfied with the answer he had received. He spoke with Amara for a few more minutes and dropped the call.

Philip typically would retreat to Social Media after such depressing encounters. A broken home. Something he could in no way change. A broken home. Something that was not his fault. If she had said he was not polished enough for her, he could have argued it was something he could learn. If she had said he was not well built he could work on that. Bad breath? Oversized shoes or shirts? Too tall? Too short? maybe he could have done something about any of these shortcomings. But coming from a broken home? What could he have done about that? Absolutely nothing!

He noticed Lara online and placed a Skype call. The discussion was filled with Amarachi and sympathies from Lara. She was always sympathetic even though she was not in a relationship herself. He hardly ever talked about her own challenges. It was easy to see that most of the time his attention was in a certain direction: on himself.

84

The Car is Mine

"Whoever has no rule over his own spirit Is like a city broken down, without walls." Proverb 25:28

Zainab's had travelled to Nigeria. It would have been her fourth week in Ghana. Philip felt like an abandoned baby. Hardly was he able to stay home after work. The Volkswagen Touareg V6 Sport made engaged him in very pleasant cruises late into the night when Accra's roads were least busy. 280 hp, 17-inch Sima wheels, Bi-Xenon headlights, all-wheel-drive, 8-speed auto-transmission. The machine just had to be used. it was purchased brand new, moonlight blue in colour, worth showing off. Simply being seen coming out of this enigma anywhere in town earned him some respect. There was a disturbing twist to his evening trips though: he was often alone or with a single lady. One would have thought he would want to go with friends and enjoy platonic evenings like most single folk his age looking for genuine relationships. If he wasn't visiting, he was alone and when alone, he made new friends.

Was he hiding something about his movements? Possibly. He would never go out of his way seeking out questionable activities or places at night, but he did come across some fringes of what a typical Christian would consider *appearances of evil* when he passed by Vienna City on his way to Nsikan beach on High Street, when he drove through Lagos street, East Legon or Oxford Street,

Osu. These locations did not mean much during the day but in the region of ten or eleven P.M. it was almost guaranteed that Philip would run into skimpily dressed ladies who wanted a lift home; often his own home not theirs. That was way across the line for him. One would wonder whether his line was at the correct position given his personal history and background.

On the night he met Victoria, he was not driving through any of these "red zones". It had been one of those hectic days when he closed from work four hours after most of his colleagues. He was not very far from home when he passed by a five-foot six size ten figure-eight lady in her late twenties standing by the bus stop. She had short hair and was wearing a simple striped long sleeve shirt and a pair of dirty jeans. Nothing really provocative. Her handbag was by her side and she looked quite pensive. On glancing at her as he passed he noticed she followed the car with her eyes and he felt the urge to stop. He did. Why did he stop? Maybe he was led by the Spirit. Maybe he felt she needed help. Maybe he needed company and knew he was not going to find any at home. Maybe he missed Zainab and wanted some temporary replacement. Whatever the reason was, he stopped. He stopped for a total stranger and had absolutely no plan about what he was going to do with the possible outcomes of his first step. Where could she be going? Would she want to sleep over? Why was she there at this time of the night? He made the decision to stop very abruptly and those few seconds between their eyes meeting and his stopping were certainly not sufficient for any detailed analysis of his decision to stop. He simply stopped. Spontaneity? Maybe. Stupidity. Well....

She walked towards the car gracefully as if she had expected him to stop. He watched her approach through the rear-view mirror and unlocked the doors as soon as she was there. She did not open, but stuck her head through the open window.

"Hi" she started.

"Hello"

There was a pause as though Philip was trying to decipher what he was supposed to say next. He must have seen this scene in a movie sometime in the past. A young single man picking up a stranger in the middle of the night. Love at first sight. Or was it just hormones making trouble in two normal humans at the right time of the night under the right circumstances. Who knew, maybe this was the way in which he would meet his future spouse. Deep in his spirit he knew it was not likely to happen that way. True love is built on genuine friendship. But how are friendships built? You have to meet someone don't you?

"Which way are you going?", Philip began.

"Korle-bu please..."

"Korlebu"

Korlebu. Now the trouble had begun. Korle-bu was minutes away. What was she going to do there at this time of the night?

"Yes please. My aunt is in hospital. Please can you help me?"

"OK."

'My aunt is in hospital'. That gave Philip the sense of duty required for him to drive thirty minutes away from home at 22:30HRS; he was helping this lady get to her aunt. This could be a life or death situation. It was worth it. Maybe he could even preach to her on the way there. Who knew.

"My name is Philip, what's yours?" Philip asked as soon as he spun the alloy wheels of the blue Touareg.

"Victoria"

"Nice. You live around here?"

"Not at all. I live at Mallam. I came through here because it was difficult to get a straight *trotro* [4] to Korlebu. I have suffered this night"

Philip could tell from her accent and expressions that she could not have gone much further than SHS. She looked simple too, no makeup, no special body cream apparently.... Her hair was short but seemed to have been curled possibly two months before, the dirty brown hue gave her away. He wondered to himself why he often met ladies who some would consider not in his class intellectually. Maybe because he was not deliberate in his search, maybe because he was not very sure what his actual requirements were. maybe because he simply was not ready for a lifelong commitment to a single person. There was too much adventure in him for that!

---

[4] Local expression for minibus in Accra

"Where do you live?"

"Just around the corner. I was on my way home..."

Victoria smiled. "Thank you very much"

Philip noticed she lowered her eyelids and eventually her face though he was not looking directly at her. That expression reminded him of what actresses do in Nigerian movies when they are supposed to be mimicking a village girl's bashfulness.

The road was as free as Philip had expected. As he made the right turn onto the stretch on which the hospital stood, he noticed the characteristic busyness of the Korle-bu neighbourhood. There was always activity this side of town, whatever time of day it was. The loud music, horns blaring and folk milling around the hospital. He slowed down as he drove through the hospital's gate parking skillfully on the red clay-gravel mix that formed the ground where the General Out Patient Department stood.

Victoria prepared herself to step out of the car.

"Hope you will wait for me?" she asked pleadingly, looking straight into his eyes as if she wanted to detect signs of dishonesty.

"Oh! OK"

Philip hadn't expected that. This favour was turning into an obligation. He could no longer refuse. 'Interesting how forward some ladies can be,' he thought to himself. 'You asked for it', said the other voice.

89

"Promise?". She looked straight into his eyes, again.

"Yes." Philip glanced at his wrist watch, regretting his benevolence and wondering what could come out of this adventure.

"I will leave my bag in the car," Victoria continued. She appeared to have a trust problem or maybe she was much smarter than she seemed. She trusted him not to leave with her bag at least but did not trust him to keep his promise to wait. Philip laughed to himself as she stepped out. She certainly was interesting. On the other hand, maybe, there was nothing very valuable in the bag after all. Pads, handkerchiefs, make-up items.... Maybe she could afford to lose all that but not her trip back to town. He caught himself following her with his eyes as she walked into the building some fifteen meters away. The bright fluorescent lighting in the porch made all the activity quite visible. Nurses walking back and forth, patients lying on benches, and a few people standing around looking tired, sad, depressed or maybe just stressed. Philip increased the inclination of the driver's seat and relaxed. He moved the seat backup and tried to stretch. He certainly could use a good bed. He suddenly recalled he had picked up some dinner of sorts - freshly made fish and chips. Fresh but cold. He had picked up the order almost an hour before. He was not in the mood for food right then.

He had waited for about ten minutes when he noticed a familiar figure approaching his SUV. He had picked her up in front of a large church a few months before. She turned out a very pleasant and decent girl and they became friends after that. She worked at Korle-bu Teaching Hospital as a nurse. He never got over why she herself agreed to get into a stranger's car at 9:05 PM at night back

90

then. Maybe she thought he was coming out of the church that evening. It was incredible how Philip always wondered why most ladies, born again or not, agreed to be picked up in a brand new, $40,000 air-conditioned SUV but never asked himself why he picked them up. If he did not intend to consummate the encounter either legally or illegally, why pick them up? In Ama's case, however, it turned out to be a very rewarding friendship. She had her expectations and once in a while asked him to visit her at the nurse's quarters, or take her out, but he did not go further than that.

"Hellooooo", she called out excitedly typical of her. Her dimpled smile was infectious, and she never lacked one on her smooth chocolate face. She never lacked words to say to him either, so the conversations were always exciting but never romantic and never sexual.

"What are you doing here?"

"How are you, Ama?", Philip stood and held her tight in an embrace. She was about a foot shorter and he seemed to swallow her up in their frequent embraces whenever they saw each other.

"I could never miss your car!". They laughed.

"So, what are you doing here at this time of the night? Hope all is well?"

"Yeah. A friend of mine came to see the aunt so I thought to help out"

91

Ama noticed he avoided using words that could give away the gender of this friend of her friend's and decided to stay the line of questioning that might make him more uncomfortable. She still had the smile on.

"How nice. Well, I am on night duty as usual..."

"How is it going? It has been long since I laid eyes on you, you know."

"You have dumped me now!" she laughed.

"How is work yourself?" Ama continued. "Hope all is well?"

"We are doing great."

"When next are you taking us out?"

Philip laughed again. It amazed him how free they had become with each other in just a few months. She had called him up more than once late at night to drop her at home after some of her church meetings. She never came to his place though but was willing to receive him at her house once in a while. To her he was a great friend and possible suitor. To him she was a great friend.

"Soon"

"OK. We are waiting...". She winked and stretched out to take hold of his hand. She was still smiling, elated. Silence for a few seconds. Then she got a call and reached for the phone in the deep pocket of the scrub she was wearing, the call lasted half a minute and she was ready to get back to work.

"...See you then..." were her words. Still smiling, she hugged him again, swallowed up by his large figure.

"OK. Mmhhh"

"And wash your hands when you get home. Ha ha ha."

Ama had disappeared into the building just as Victoria showed up at the door. They must have missed each other by inches. Victoria walked briskly towards Philip wearing her won infectious smile, elated that Philip was there, waiting for her.

"I'm back!" she announced with glee.

Philip simply smiled, still reminiscing on his chance encounter with Ama. What could have happened if she had met Victoria? What needed to happen? She was not his girlfriend, was she? That was Philip's safety net: no commitments! It was more acutely put 'No spoken commitments'. Women typically interpret actions and translate them to words in their head, patiently waiting for the men that have been speaking with actions to finally voice out. When the man's actions change, it is probably as much a heart break as if he had actually made a spoken commitment. Philip had spoken to a lot of women and yet not spoken to any of them. His speech problem would finally result in a series of issues when he finally decides to speak to one of them.

As they sat in the car and got set to go, Philip snapped out of his trance briefly:

"How is your Aunt doing?"

93

"Fine ooo. She will be out of hospital on Thursday."

"Good"

"Will you come and pick me?"

Philip cringed. This lady was definitely too hot to handle. Asking for another pickup when the first uncomfortable one was not yet concluded.

"I am not sure. Let's see..."

Did he just tell a lie? Not exactly. A short silence and Victoria spoke up again. He could easily have named her Petra, the female apostle of Jesus who could not keep quiet for too long. She had adjusted her body a bit, facing him and resting her right thigh slightly over her left. Her cleavage was clearly visible through her shirt which had two top buttons open.

"Can we go to your place?"

"My place?" Philip's heart began to beat faster. Thoughts started racing through his head. His place? He could not afford that. This lady was just too strong for him, too uncultured, too forward. He would definitely not be able to control her.

"Another time," Philip concluded, keeping calm. Another lie.

"Why?"

Victoria had thought this was going somewhere. Why would he not want to take her home or even to bed. Everyone does it and this was a big fish. She would not let him go without a fight. Philip took a brief glance at her.

"Why do you want to go to my house? Isn't it late?"

Victoria looked away. What kind of naivety was this? She did not go to the university like him, but she was certainly much smarter streetwise, she thought to herself. Was she supposed to spell it out.

"OK. Just show me where it is"

Her countenance had dropped. Like a drowning man grabbing anything and everything, she was not struggling with him. 'I do not need to enter, just show me the house'. Philip though about it. His inclination to please everyone tugged at his throat. he could not bear offending this nice young lady. In a few more minutes he parked in front of his gate.

"Which one is it?" she asked, disappointed.

"This... " Philip pointed carelessly at his house. She didn't believe him.

"OK." Victoria was not smiling anymore. "So, will you take me home?"

It was almost 12:30 AM and she did not seem perturbed. She was obviously used to night life expecting a total stranger to drive her eleven kilometres at 12:30 AM in the morning.

"Do you live with your parents?"

"No. My sister."

"I see. Would she not be worried if she sees you being dropped by a man?"

Victoria laughed.

"But men drop her too now, besides she knows where I went. I even called her from my Aunty's bedside. And I am an adult, why should she be worried."

"I see."

After a few minutes of silence, Philip called a truce.

"I will drop you off at Kaneshie. Will you get a bus there?"

"At this time, I don't know o. I can pick a taxi"

"OK"

"You will give me some money for transport, right?"

Philip could not believe what he had gotten himself into. Money? Even Zainab never asked him for money. He drove into a petrol station at *Obetsebi Lamptey Circle* and stepped out of the SUV. This night ride was getting sour.

"Where are you going?" Victoria yelled.

"ATM" he called back without stopping. He was back in three minutes and handed her Fifty Cedis without looking at her. She stared at it for a few seconds and blurted out:

"It won't be enough?"

"What?" Philip almost burst out of his physical body. This was just too much. 'Not enough?'. She wasn't about to cook a meal for him, was she. Whose fault was this. She must have raised her voice then:

"Philp why are you treating me like this now? Why? Are you going to drop me here and leave me stranded? it is not fair o. It is not fair!"

Philip chose the path of caution. He was right. He could not control this lady. he gently dipped his fingers into his pocket and picked another fifty-cedi note. She thanked him in a softer tone before the money got into her hands. But the smile was gone. Maybe she would have got a lot more if she had left his house six hours later.

The door was still open. The bright lights from the petrol station partly lit up the interior of the car and the engine and car radio were both talking. Once in a while a late-night driver on the express interrupted the quad briefly. Amidst the public privacy, Philip instinctively reached out and stroked her left breast with the back of his index finger then searched with his eyes for a response in her face. The red was there. No more smiles, no more anger just bright red faces longing for something that was so hard to give particularly on Philip's part. He shut his door and turned off the engine, amplifying the privacy. He reached out again and held on to her nipple softly. She broke into a shy smile.

"Let's go to your house" she whispered. He ignored her and reached for her right hand pulling it towards his right lap. Soon she felt his ascent. She pushed his hand gently away from her breast, he asked why without speaking, merely looking into her face quizzically.

"Blue balls..." she blurted.

"What?"

"You will get blue balls"

"What is that?"

She paused. How does a twenty-seven-year-old girl explain blue balls to a thirty-something year old man? She ventured, speaking softly and deliberately as if she was explaining something to a little child.

"When you stir up yourself and you don't have sex you get pains in your private part". She looked deep into his face as if she would have asked 'Do you want sex or not?'. He certainly did not want sex, a virgin at thirty-three, he was not about to fail God now. But had he not already failed? And that virgin matter? Was he really a virgin? He himself was not so sure.

Lagos Nigeria, Early 80s

Philip was less than six years old, but he remembered the incident like the colour of his left hand. Mgborie, his mother's third house help, a fourteen-year-old girl over a series of weeks had taught him what to do to excite her sexually. Who would have guessed something like that was going on under his parent's noses, in a house full of people? Philip learnt what to do without knowing what he was doing up to the point of penetration. He remembered the smell on his finger when he touched her lower parts, the hair, the warmth. the memories made the thought of sexual intercourse with any woman abhorrent. Utterly abhorrent. But it did not take his hormones away even. Neither did his faith in Jesus Christ.

Blue balls. Philip pulled away and started the engine. Just when he was about to drop Victoria off they exchanged numbers. Why? If he could answer that question, then he would also have to answer all the others. Why did he pick her? Why did he take her all the way to Korlebu? Why did he touch her nipple? Why? Not everything can be explained. Not everything makes sense. Some things are just better forgotten.

As soon as he stepped into his living room those early hours, he heard the Silent Whisper "That was such a waste of time don't you think?". He ignored the Voice. He was ever so gentle. And why did His voice seem so distant during the actual close calls? Was He far away at those moments or were Philip's ears simply deafened temporarily? He could not sleep till about 3:00 AM. Depression. He finally slept off on the living room couch, while the television was on. He sought of missed Zainab. He woke up at 6:00 AM thinking about Ama and Victoria. Then Zainab, Abena and Helen. He remembered the last time he gave strangers a lift. He never did get their names.

He had been roaming Adabraka out of boredom that quiet Sunday evening. As he left the petrol station he passed two plump looking, light complexioned ladies, heavily made up and well-dressed asides the fact that their skirts went just over half way down their femurs. One was a little taller than the other but on the whole, no one would describe any of them as particularly tall. He went pass for about five meters then turned back. A taxi had also stopped in front of them but one of them had been watching Philip's car so she tapped her companion and they let the taxi go.

"Which way are you going?" Philip had asked.

"East Legon"

9:30 PM. East Legon. Just about 30 minutes away. Not a bad idea.

"I can drop you...", Philip finally said.

He realized from their accent that they were Igbos. He turned on the air conditioner and rolled up the glasses. Then he switched on the radio to 94.3 FM. A worship song was playing, and he joined silently. Then he decided to start a conversation.

"How was church today?" He asked out of the blues.

One of the ladies, the shorter one had sat in the front seat. She seemed to be the team lead. She appeared more in control, more vocal. She answered him.

"Fine, Sir"

"What church do you attend?"

"Pure Fire."

It was a well-known church with a sound minister as the general Overseer. Philip pondered on the implications. They were obviously prostitutes; how did they survive weekly preaching at this church. Why did they bother going in the first place? It was puzzling to him. Sometimes men want God in their lives, but they just cannot let go of things that God may not want in their lives. But who was he to judge? He had his own skeletons, didn't he?

He paused a bit and wondered how best to proceed. On this particular evening despite his loneliness and carelessness in picking up woman on the street, he felt particularly spiritually powerful. There was no desire for intercourse, no lust, no flirting, just a very calm disposition as he spoke to these two plump ladies in their late thirties.

"Let me share what I learnt in church today and then you can also share yours," he began.

"OK. No wahala..."

It was still the team lead responding though Philip noticed through his rear-view mirror that the other lady was also paying attention. Maybe she was already convicted of her sins as she realized they had been picked up by a Christian brother. The team lead must have been 'already hardened in sin' Philip had thought to himself.

"The preacher spoke about life being like an examination... and every choice we have to make in our lives being like an exam question..."

He paused. Waiting for the statement to sink in. Reaching out with his feelers to see whether he was getting through or getting resistance. He continued:

"...we choose how we answer each question and they add up. At the end the papers are marked, and we are given our rewards..."

"Salvation is not by works o... " the lady cut in.

"True. But when we are saved there is a certain quality of life that God expects from us. *'And every man that hath this hope in him purifieth himself, even as he is pure'* I John 3:3. Have you read that before?"

She was not so quick to answer. "No. I am not so good in reading Bible, but I know God very well. He has done a lot of things for me..."

It is amazing how many people know the basics of grace. Philip could not condemn her, could he? It hurt him however how it was possible for a person to consistently live in sin and have a systematic defense for their lifestyle apparently based on teaching they had received from church. It always made him wonder whether the charismatic church was getting things right. Philip cut in:

"Have you read Revelation 20:12 '... and the dead were judged out of those things which were written in the books, according to their works' or Galatians 5:21 '... of the which I tell you before, as I have also told you in time past, that they which do such things shall not inherit the kingdom of God'"

"You might be quoting these things out of context o. We are saved by grace. 'He that is without sin let him cast the first stone'!"

Philip would have laughed out loud if the discussion was not so serious. She was right in that he had no right to cast stones. But here she was using the scriptures to avoid facing a clear reality that there may be things in her life she needs to let go of. She did not even want to let any kind of conviction set in. Philip looked in the rear-view mirror and realized the other lady was paying attention and he just kept talking till they got to Lagos Road on the way to Ajirigano. He did not quite recognize the place, but it seemed to be a restaurant or night club of sorts. Both ladies stepped out and thanked him as he maneuvered the large SUV making a u-turn they just stared at him. What kind of young single man would have this kind of car and preach like this? Philip heard the Silent Whisper "I am proud of you!"

All this had run through his head that morning as he set out for work, his head aching from a very short night. Victoria called him later that morning and he picked, spoke to her coldly for a few minutes and excused himself to stop the call when she began asking for a lift to pick her aunt. He never answered her calls again.

"Which kain man be dat?" Nneka asked.

"I neva see before o. Im no even look your side at all" answered Amaka.

Nneka gave her friend a sharp look which turned Amaka's laugh switch to ten points. "Which kain talk be dat? Na your side im come look, abi?"

Amaka reached out to playfully hold her while still cackling with laughter but Nneka pushed her away and moved on away from the T-junction where they had been dropped and towards the noisy, dimly lit bar. Amaka followed a foot or two behind and added salt to injury:

"Im dey use di mirror dey look me oh" She stuck out her tongue briefly while Nneka was not looking and kept laughing.

Suddenly they were both quiet. Something seemed to have struck both of them at about the same instant. Amaka was especially hit. She began to speak:

"But Nneka, dis ting wey we de do so, when we go stop am? God fit dey vex for us o.."

"Nne *biko* [5]just face ya work abeg. Na im go give you food chop? Im don preach finish dey go. Im give you *shishi*[6]? Im don chop beleful dey preach na. You know wetin im done do before im come dey preach?"

---

[5] Igbo word for "Please"
[6] Expression implying a very tiny amount

104

"Nneka dis wan wey you dey talk be 'by di bush o'. God dey vex, *kponkwen*[7] "

When conviction comes to us, we can argue and rationalize all we want but that uncomfortable feeling lingers and just will not go away. It is there whether our sins are visible to others or not. The feeling is worse when our sins are not visible to others. We choose what to do with those nudging of the Silent Whisper. He is willing to wait for extensive periods of time for our response. He keeps hoping we eventually respond correctly.

[7] Igbo word for "full stop" or end of a matter

Clash of the Concubines

"And in that day seven women shall take hold of one man, saying,
'We will eat our own food and wear our own apparel;
Only let us be called by your name,
To take away our reproach.'" Isaiah 4:1

"So, what do you think?"

"He is nice. So, has he spoken?"

Abena hesitated. "Well... not in many words...". She kept her eyes on the picture she had been showing her colleague, Sandra when the banking hall was less busy.

"So, you are just friends?"

"Yup"

"Hmm... Have you slept with him yet?"

Abena gave her a disgusted look which made her laugh. Sandra looked away, a sinister smile still perched on her face. She attended to a customer and turned her attention back to Abena.

"You didn't answer the question"

"Sandra, you know I have more respect for my body than that!"

"I hear! Holy Mary, Mother of God"

"Sandra don't do that!" She gave a very serious look. Her respect for Mary was more serious to her than the Holy Spirit was to most Charismatic Christians. She just could not allow anyone around her to make fun of the *Blessed Virgin Mary.* She glanced at the clock straight ahead across the waiting area and noticed they had about twenty minutes to close of business. Two back office staff walked across the waiting area on their way out blocking her view for a few seconds. She beckoned on a customer to step forward as soon as the view was clear again.

Sandra had that smirk on her face again and started talking:

"So, what are you going to do?"

"Do? About what?"

"How are you going to get him?"

"Get who? I am not interested"

Abena cleared her throat. Sandra laughed again.

"You are always pretending to have it all together. These days you don't have to be all lady-like else you will age single! I can see you like the guy so make him love you. Some guys need a little push. Or are you worried that he is a Nigerian? Nigerians are very romantic o"

"Is that so," Abena mocked, "So how many of them have romanced you?"

Sandra used the handkerchief on her of her next round of laughter. She could easily have turned every head in the office in her direction with that outburst.

"Look Sandra, I am not like you. And I don't see any benefit of being like you anyway because it has not gotten you a permanent man has it?"

"*Adein*[8]? And who says I am looking for a permanent man? Enjoy life while you are young! I am barely twenty-seven and you are talking about a permanent man?"

"I definitely do not want your advice then!"

"But you want Philip, right?"

Silence.

Both ladies started getting ready to close.

After a little more silence Sandra burst into a chuckle non-stop. Both were going through the cycle of leaning over to pick up bundles of notes, counting them and binding them in hundreds. Abena ignored her at first but could not bear it any longer after she chuckled the third time. She looked out of her cubicle and blurted "Sandra behave yourself!"

---

[8] Twi for "Why"

"Stop pretending. You will die of sex starvation o"

"Sandra!"

She simply laughed.

"Abena stop pretending and enjoy life. You are not Mother Mary!"

Abena sat up suddenly and made a serious looking face. "Sandra behave yourself. Leave Mother out of this!"

It was about six thirty when both ladies finally started leaving the complex. The Back-Office staff had taken over. It was almost completely dark but the street along which they had to walk to get to the car park some thirty meters away was relatively busy with people. North Ridge was not completely shut down till about 8:30 PM on most days. The walk was fast paced and chatty for the most part between the two. Every now and then the trees made the walkway a little darker than it really was, blocking out the sparse street lights.

"... But are you sure he doesn't have a girlfriend?"

"How would I know? Our relationship is not like that. But I think he would have told me if he did. He tells me a lot and I do too. We are good friends"

"But he is not going to be available forever o. So, if you want him, you had better make a move if he is not making a move."

Abena did not answer. Sandra kept talking.

"Me I have my plans. Once I find the man I really like I will just have a child with him! There is no need to tie myself down with marriage. It is such a hassle"

Abena stared at her friend.

"A hassle! Sandra, you are just a case! Marriage is a responsibility. It is the best environment to really show that you love someone despite their shortcomings. Life is not only about fun. Get serious."

Sandra simply made a gesture as though she tapped the surface of a drum with the tip of her fingers. "O Come off it! Have you checked out married folk these days? Who is happily married. No one! Do not deceive yourself. Better beware before you get trapped. Once trapped, societal pressure will not let you off easily..."

"Free? Free to do what? Free to have sex with every Tom, Dick and Harry?"

"I do not sleep with every man I see o. I am free to choose which I sleep with and when. It all depends on my mood. I know you are a virgin but when you experience sex you will realize that one man cannot satisfy you no matter how hard he tries!"

A film of fluid welled up in Abena's eyes. She was not particularly emotional, but she did have her moments. This was one of those moments. Why did it have to feel so out of place? yes, she was a virgin and she wanted to keep herself for her husband but crossing the thirty border still "innocent" was sometimes embarrassing. Why was it embarrassing? Because everyone else in her age group, married or unmarried, experienced sex every now and then as a regular part of their lives. Husbands, boyfriends, one-night-stands etc. Every lady around her had someone "keeping them happy". Was she happy? Yes, she was. She did not need sex to make her happier. Or maybe she did not even know she could be happier... with sex.

"So, many men keep you happy?"

Now Sandra was quiet for a change. For a second. Abena glanced at her.

"You just have to keep trying"

Happiness. A state of being or a brief experience. What is the relationship between happiness and ecstasy? Does ecstasy create happiness? Does a momentary thrilling experience create a happy person, or does it take a series of ecstatic experiences? It almost sound like drug use. Heroine. Cocaine. Multiple injections or inhalations are required to keep the high daily. Sex. Multiple encounters a week are required to maintain the "happiness". Someone is keeping all the ladies happy. That is three or four times a week!

"Give me your phone"

"My phone? Why"

"Let me check something..."

"Check what? I am not giving you any phone!"

Abena's phone was visible in her large handbag. Sandra took her off guard, grabbed her handbag and ran across the street narrowly missing a moving car. Abena could not cross immediately. Her fingers quickly danced around the keypad and she had arrived at Philip's contact details in seconds just before Abena had a chance to cross safely.

"Hi Philip, are you still in the office, we are coming over..."

Abena grabbed the phone and continued the call.

"Hello Abena, yes I'm here. Why are you talking so fast?"

"Philip..."

Contemplation. She could easily have called it off as a friend's prank, but it would do no harm to see him. What would she be going all the way home to do any way....

"Yeah. You can come by. I can take you home"

"To your place or?"

"Oh. Abena... OK."

"Ha ha ha. I was joking o. "

" I hear. Alright. See you soon"

Abena ended the call and looked at Sandra. She had a huge smile on her face. Abena turned away from her and started walking towards the car park. Sandra stepped forward and hugged her from behind refusing to let go while Abena struggled.

"C'mon leave me alone. Naughty girl!'

Sandra laughed. The Toyota Corolla was close. It still had the shiny teal colour. It was bought brand new with a staff loan. Abena was not interested in any kind of loan so she preferred to save for hers. Sandra always dropped her off at Abeka Junction and she would complete the journey home herself in a taxi, today was different. She would take her to see Philip... at the office. Maybe there would be a trip home too. That sounded exciting to Abena, but she would not show it. Exciting because it made her feel closer to him not because she wanted to be happy for a few minutes like her Sandra every now and then. What did she really want from him? A relationship. Marriage? Not necessarily. Just a relationship. A romantic relationship? Not necessarily. Just a relationship. The workings of a woman's mind will always be complex. Men misinterpret all the time and make moves that mar the relationship. The difference between 'like' and 'love' seems very clear to a woman even though they cannot articulate same in words. The difference is unclear to a man. The case of Fuzzy Logic versus Boolean Algebra.

Labone. A good portion of Accra's upper middle class built their homes here. A large portion of that portion were foreigners - mostly modern Asians who had taken over the business landscape of Accra from big supermarkets to IT. The roads were just perfect: wide, sparkling clean and almost brand new. The embassies and consulates were here too. The banks built their structures here with class as though they had more respect for the name Labone than they had for Lartebiokoshie or New Town or Bubuashie. Some things were good in Ghana and Labone was one of them. Philip's office was located here amongst the other high-profile outfits owned by foreigners. Labone was different from a lot of other places for another reason too: nothing was difficult to find once you had the address. They could not have found *Kolours* so easily in many other parts of Accra: Adabraka, Kaneshie, Kotobabi etc. Maybe it would have been equally as easy if it was sited at North Ridge, Roman Ridge, Airport Residential and the like. The disparities in African cities were here in Accra too.

The car park was just about full. The smiling security guard in a white top, black bottom semi-military outfit helped her park adjacent an already parked Skoda Octavia. She glanced at it when they stepped out of the car. Very nice car, a little old though. 2008? Maybe.

"Let's go, Abena"

Abena looked up at the building. A five-storey beauty covered in glass. She was sure those inside could see everything happening outside. maybe even Philip would see her and hurry downstairs. Fancy that. The open area used as a car park was as bright as day with flood lights and the like. This car park must have been like three quarters full. Cars were neatly parked along white markings on the smooth concrete floor. The workers here were obviously not as enthusiastic about going home as bankers were, were they? She noticed the gadgets on the penthouse. Maybe a radio station or ISP also used this building. Certainly, up to four outfits must have shared this edifice. In this part of Accra, high rise buildings were not all that popular so this one seemed particularly imposing at five storeys.

Sandra was more enthusiastic about this trip than her friend. She led the way to hunt down Philip Ezeani. At the reception they waited for Rebecca to place a call to Philip's floor. Just then Helen, on her way home, stepped out of the lift and overheard the enquiry. She looked at Abena. Abena could not help noticing her flowing white gown spotted with green leaves and pink flowers on one side. That kind of dressing was certainly not something a banker like her could wear to work on any day of the week. Their eyes locked till it could easily be defined as a stare. They communicated even though they had never seen each other. Sandra was busy with the receptionist, Rebecca. She tapped Abena out of her standoff with Helen and they sat down.

"Who was that?"

"I don't know"

"So why were you staring at her?"

Sandra examined Abena's face as if she was looking for traces of dishonesty.

"Well... she was staring so I stared back. Some people are just plain rude! You see someone you don't know at a reception and start staring..."

"Maybe she likes your suit!"

Both women laughed hard. Abena broke the frenzy, "You are in someone's office o"

A few blocks away as Helen walked to her car she called Philip. They had not spoken for weeks except for brief moments when tasks in the office brought them together. She would hardly look into his face these days, so it was surprising that she called. He hesitated and then picked up the call.

"Helen?" He tried to be pleasant, but his alarm could not be hidden.

"Your girlfriends are outside. Hope they have told you!"

"Girlfriends?"

"Your bank girlfriends!"

Philip could tell from the tone of her voice that this was not going to be a pleasant call if he continued the discussion.

"OK..." Philip concluded calmly.

Helen dropped the call fighting tears. She was angry. Like a wife whose husband had been taken away from her by a younger woman. Like a heart broken bride whose husband never showed up. She felt totally ignored. She could not believe how much she wanted him.

Her car had been blocked and she confronted the smiling security guard.

"Whose car is this?" She hollered pointing at the teal Toyota Corolla.

"Sorry Madam. let me get the keys."

He clumsily rummaged through a plastic contained where he and his colleagues had been keeping car keys for a minute or two before it dawned on him that he had forgotten to collect the keys from the two ladies whom he had helped park. His smile gradually faded.

"Madam, sorry. I will get the keys right now..."

He walks briskly towards the reception apologizing to Helen in a shaky voice. She hissed and went after him in much more measured steps.

"Madam sorry. Please Madam... " He was calling out to Sandra and Abena just about the time the chime from the lift's opening doors filled the reception area. Both ladies turned.

"Madam sorry. The other madam wants to move, and you are blocking her..."

Sandra paused. Abena cut in.

"You can just give him the keys to help you move it."

"Like seriously? No o. I will move it myself. You can go ahead"

"Oh! No. I will wait for you"

As though the lift had heard, the doors shut, and it started moving back up again. Sandra step out through the revolving doors. She was greeted again by the floodlights that had turned the entire area into day in the midst of night. She could make out Helen who had stopped half way between the front door and the parked cars. She was leaning against Philip's Touareg. If Sandra had known Philip's car she could have guessed what that stare was really about. Abena saw her from inside and smiled. So that was the issue!

"What nonsense is this? How can you come in here and just block someone's car and take away the car key?" Helen attacked.

Sandra stopped. She was about three feet away from Sandra but her voice could be heard as far as the reception and the security house in the other direction.

"What?" Sandra whispered. Shocked. Abena's eyes widened. She was more worried for Helen than for Sandra. Sandra was the kind that could take her suit off and engage in physical combat with anyone anywhere. She never did in the office simply because she needed the constant flow of money from a bank job.

"Please come and move this stack of junk let me go home!"

"Are you OK? Who do you think you are? Are you drunk or something?"

Sandra was still speaking in normal tones. Kwame, the Security Guard was now playing the intermediary and his colleagues had come to the scene after the first outburst. Kwame tried to get the keys out of Sandra's hands.

"Sorry Ma. Don't worry Ma. I will help you move your car. Don't worry..."

Sandra gave him a look that made him drop his hands quickly. "Please move"

She moved towards Helen who was still standing close to Philip's Touareg. Sandra's heavy figure ought to have made Helen, a size eight, wary about having a face-off with her. Sandra moved towards Helen and noticed the defiance in her face. She gave her a soft push. The security men tried to hold her back.

"Look! Small girl! If you try me this evening I will wake you up from whatever they have given you to drink, better shut up and go play with your mates! Nonsense"

Four men struggled to hold Sandra back. It was such an interesting scene for those who loved to watch others fight. A fight was brewing here between two women. It was one of those awkward moments when a quarrel breaks out and someone who is smart enough realizes there is more to it than the little step on the toe that was visible to everyone. There was certainly more to this matter than the fact that Sandra had blocked Helen's car. Even the security guards knew.

Abena was close. She had been walking briskly towards Philip's car. She knew that car quite well. Maybe this slim lady had deliberately chose to stand by it for this face off.

"Sandra!"

"Abena come and see this mosquito..."

"Bundle her away! If not, I will call the police!" Helen could not be silenced. Her eyes widened. She kept her distance but kept raising her voice, threatening and insulting the ladies, sweating profusely while at it.

119

"Madam, what is this about? Is it just the car or something else?" Abena asked. She did not wait for an answer.

"Sandra please let me have the keys. Let's go"

"Who is your Madam? Idiot!" Helen snapped. Sizing her with disdain in her eyes. Abena heard the words faintly, she had turned her attention away towards Sandra.

Abena managed to drag Sandra away with a little help from the dumbfounded security guards. This time she drove. She had just crossed the gate, giving the guards time to burst out in a round of laughter in their 'office' when it was as though Sandra's frenzy resumed:

"Oh God, Oh God!" She yelled, "Abena you should have let me deal with that mosquito! What nonsense. She doesn't know her size. O!"

Abena kept quiet. She was visibly angry. Not at the slim, stylish young woman who had embarrassed them in front of Philip's office and not at Philip himself. She was angry at herself for letting this trip to his office happen in the first place. She vowed to herself not to let it happen again. That little lady would not have had the effrontery to initiate that face off of if there was nothing going on between them. Office Wife! Her phone rang. Sandra picked the call and put the phone on her right cheek.

"Hi Abena. Where are you?" It was Philip.

"I left."

"Left? What's wrong?" He was standing by his car. Helen had long gone right behind the ladies and Philip was turning his head back and forth in the now scanty car park looking for Abena as though she would be hidden under one of the ten to twelve cars now left at the front of the brightly lit car park.

Abena hesitated and then let it out: "Your office wife chased us away. I guess she was afraid we were coming to snatch her husband!"

"What?"

"I am driving! I will talk to you later... Bye."

"Ok." The line was dead before he finished the two-letter word.

Abena was pensive. Sandra was silent. maybe this was her fault after all. how could she have known the young man was some kind of philanderer knocking women's heads together. The way Abena spoke about him it was as if she had him all to herself, but no one had Philip. Philip had himself and managed to give those he cared about their portion of his time. The time allocated to each lady was good enough to satisfy them and position them as very dear to him. Perception is everything.

It was in no way deliberate, he was not really trying to knock heads together. He was not trying to have all the ladies. One could even claim they were trying to have him. He was just being nice, and he did care about each princess in his 'harem'. He just did not consider any of them his girlfriend or anything close to that. Girlfriend? No! not even Zainab.

Helen was still on the road when Philip called. She picked the call using her Bluetooth device.

"Hi Philip. Surprise, surprise. I thought we were not talking to each other!" She sounded in high spirits though she did not smile. They say one can tell if you are smiling over the phone. The excitement in her voice could not have given away her near-death experience a few minutes previously. Philip hesitated now wondering if she was actually the one Abena had encountered. He had assumed it was her since she had called early claiming his bank girlfriends were looking for him.

"Did you meet two ladies who came to see me before you left the office?"

"Yeah...any issue?"

Should he ask this question and how should he ask it safely. He hadn't been on talking terms with Helen for weeks. If he had assumed wrong, then this would probably extend the malice another few months.

"Did you speak with them by any chance?"

Helen paused. Then spoke again, with a little less excitement.

"What did they tell you? That I fought with them? They blocked my car and I simply asked them to move. Why should they block my car? ..." The excitement was back ... in the other direction.

"So, the issue was your car?"

122

"Yes! It was my car. "

"Helen, I have not known you to be a cantankerous person. And I am even more surprised that you went public with a face off of this nature. I don't know what happened out here but the way Abena sounded, I am sure it was serious. And I have to put it on record, Helen that I am very disappointed with you"

"Disappointed, are you? Disappointed my foot! So Abena is her name, is it?" Helen noticed other drivers in traffic stealing glances at her through the sealed windows. They could not hear anything, but it was obvious she was raising her voice on the phone and she complicated it by flinging her hand in the air as she spoke.

"I should be the one disappointed in you! I thought you were a respectable gentleman. I thought you had some honour!"

"What are you talking about?"

"You led me on Philip! That's what I am talking about! And I was foolish enough to fall for it. Now you have moved to bank ladies... and they are now visiting you in the office... carry on."

"Helen..."

"Let me finish! Better tell those girls never to cross my path again... or they will pay for it. Just let them visit you at home.... alright... at home and you can do whatever you like with them there!"

"Helen, I have to drop this call. You are sounding incredulous!"

123

She heard the beep as Philip ended the call and broke into sobs. Struggling, she kept wiping her face with the tissue on her dashboard.

"Abena," she whispered, "I will get you for this. I will get you..."

Bullseye

"If you do well, will you not be accepted? And if you do not do well, sin lies at the door. And its desire is for you, but you should rule over it." Genesis 4:7

Spots of red, yellow and white light interspersed with patches of empty land littered the landscape. Zainab looked out the window. No matter how many times she saw it from the sky, the view always looked amazing. She heard the voice of the lady whose face no one ever saw, telling everyone to strap their seat belts in preparation for landing. The buckle snapped, and she glanced at the huge body builder beside her in a black T-shirt. She thought about Philip. She was going to see him again. Why was she looking forward to it so much? She missed him. Whatever this was between them was really deep and it was not going away soon.

She did not speak to anyone for any length of time while making the trip from the tarmac to the arrivals. Just a few "hellos" and smiles. The chatting and laughing of passengers, the occasional blare from the PA system, and all the other sounds typical of Kotoka International Airport seemed very far away from Zainab's ears. She thought about Philip coming to meet her at the airport. Why had he agreed to come all the way? It was almost like someone eager to see his wife returning from years living abroad. It was a great feeling, to be bound to someone so strongly, so naturally yet so inexplicably. She could not understand the feelings that were at play in her heart. Did she love him? Did he love her? What would become of them once her program was over? What was the definition of their relationship?

At the arrivals, Philip stared at the electronic board watching for the line declaring the arrival of the evening flight from Lagos. He had been eagerly going over the lines from top to bottom, looking for the key word 'Lagos'. It wasn't long before she came through the gates clad in a pair of black jeans and white flowing blouse which went with the wind. Her brown boots were amazing, showing off her sassiness. Philip stepped out from behind the barricade, smiling eternally as he waited for her to reach him. He was about to take over the luggage when Zainab reached out and embraced him. She held on tight and he did too. Things were quiet for a few seconds between them then Zainab whispered, "I missed you..." and waited. Did he miss her too? She wanted to know. He did not speak but he held on. He could feel the rush in his hormones. He did not want to let go. Something about this lady simply captured him completely. She pulled back and Philip loosened the grip reluctantly. He felt the stare of onlookers in the crowd almost as much as he felt her hands running up his shirt towards his face. She held his face up with both her palms on his cheeks and looked straight into his eyes.

"Did you miss me too?" Zainab asked.

Philip merely nodded. The redness of his face and the look in his eyes betrayed him completely and a nod combined with these two was sufficient for Zainab. She believed he missed her too. Zainab touched his forehead with hers inches away from a kiss on the lips,

126

oblivious of the crowd. Philip pulled back gently, and reached for her luggage, breathing heavily.

The couple made their way out of the arrivals hall with Philip leading the way. He avoided eye contact with anyone. He was embarrassed. What if someone had seen him? What would they think of him. Zainab was not in the least disturbed about the opinions of others about her. She simply expressed herself the way she felt. It did not matter who was or was not looking. Philip heard whispers in the crowd, a little giggling here and there as he walked over to a counter to pay for parking. Zainab chose not to hear any of the passing comments. She was a little upset Philip had not held her hand. He walked as if he was running from her, but he was running from the stare and whispers.

Nothing much had changed at the house in Zainab's eyes. One week was not a long time, was it? As they stepped into the living room she recalled the first time she was in the same house a few weeks earlier. She recalled the first time they held each other and the nights that they spent sitting with each other all those nights. Philip was scared something worse would happen. She was scared something more would not happen. Why was Philip holding back? it was obvious he wanted something more than just cuddling. Everything seemed right, but it just wasn't right. Why did he let her come back? Why did he not complain about her having stayed over a month? The plan was one week. He definitely wanted her here but what was he going to do with her while she was here. What if nothing really happened and she moved to her own place? Would he ever come around?

The house was so quiet both of them could hear crickets chirping outside the house, horns blaring from the road side every now and then. Philip wanted the quiet, so he did not turn the TV on. He wanted to know what she was thinking. She wanted to know what he wanted. What he really wanted. They sat on the couch with one foot between them after dropping Zainab's luggage. No one spoke for any length of time. Philip noticed the glimmer on her far from a film of perspiration. It was not a particularly warm night so the sweat must have come from somewhere else. She spoke, not looking at him:

"Want to watch a movie?"

"Not really"

"So, what do you want to do?"

Philip did not respond.

"Let me shower..."

"OK"

Minutes later just as he picked up the TV remote control, Philip's phone rang. Philip realized he had left it in Zainab's room along with her things. He went for it but she met her at her door, clad in her towel. She looked at it out of curiosity. She did not recognize the name, but she turned green when she noticed it was a lady's name. Who would be calling him from Nigeria at past nine o' clock. She gave him a look as if she owned him. 'Who was Amarachi Onuoma?' she asked in her thoughts. Philip was aroused seeing her in her pink towel. It managed to cover everything from the

128

beginning of her cleavage to just a little below her pelvic area. He must have stared. When his eyes got back to her face he observed the shower cap was the same colour.

"Your phone," said Zainab.

"Oh! Thanks."

His eyes brightened when he saw Amara's name on his display. It was the third ring. She must have really wanted to talk to him.

"Where are you, Philip?". Those were her first words as he picked the phone. she was never very formal with him. They definitely would have made a great couple. Great friends make great couples.

"At home. Why? How are you though?"

"I am fine. Why did it take so long to pick up the phone, Brother?"

Philip laughed. Amara always made him laugh.

"Have you joined the KGB? What are you investigating?"

"It is the CIA I have joined, brother and I am investigating your activities!"

Philip paused. He hadn't done anything yet had he? He had thought about what would happened between him and Zainab under the circumstances given the emotional tension he could feel in the house. Or had Amara somehow heard he was living with a lady in Accra? Had the Holy Spirit told her? He was nervous.

"Philip. Are you there?"

129

"Yeah..."

"Anyway, I just thought about you and decided to call. How have you been? Hope you are not doing anything I would not do?"

Philip laughed again.

"What would you not do?"

"*Gi onwe go ma*[9]!"

"How is Naija?"

"We are fine o"

"And your family?"

"We are fine. When can I start asking you the same question?"

Philip roared with laughter. He paced in the living room as he spoke on the phone. The television was on, but he had turned the volume almost to the very bottom. He heard the shower stop as his laughter ground to a halt. Zainab was done. He was distracted a bit then spoke again.

"If you hadn't talked about marriage then I would have wondered whether it was really you."

"That is not the answer to the question, Brother."

"Don't worry I will invite you soon."

---

[9] Igbo for "You yourself know"

Zainab flashed in Philip's mind. Could she fill this gap? Even if she could, it was not supposed to happen this way? That was not the way he imagined it. How would he give the testimony to his Christian friends? Zainab came to live in his house for a month and then he found out that she was his wife? Was it providence that had led her here? What if they ended up having sex? How would his testimony go? Would he even marry her? What would happen to Abena? Helen? All the others? He was simply not ready for commitment, but he was hungry for sexual expression.

Zainab stepped in the living room. She looked clean, no makeup and no film of sweat. She wore a short nightie and had her hair bound in a scarf. She threw herself on the couch and turned her head towards the television muttering, "You are still on the phone". Philip glanced at her.

"OK o," Amara concluded, "I just thought to say hello *sha*. Take care of yourself. Have a good night's rest alone in your big house..."

"Alright. Thanks a lot"

Was that a lie? Not telling her that he was not alone? Was he supposed to correct her and say he was not alone? Philip was not so sure about that, but his own conscience and the Silent Whisper told him something was wrong with this night. Amara's call was a wakeup call.

"Come and sit with me" called Zainab.

Philip hesitated. "Let me have a bath"

"OK"

131

He recognized this variant of Zainab's voice. The soft, mellow variant. It was like cold water wetting his heart, a song inviting him closer, a silver cord that connected them both. She wanted him, and he wanted her but neither would speak about it. The body language was enough said.

The bathroom was turbulent. The turbulence was not in the water rushing from his shower. It was not in the gentle breeze troubling the grass behind his bathroom window. The turbulence was inside him. Thoughts rushed through his mind, restlessness raged in his soul, he was in a hurry to finish his bath yet nervous about all the things that could possibly happen when he got out of the bathroom and stepped into his living room where Zainab was waiting, anticipating, wondering what he would do when he finally came to sit beside her. Anticipation. Uncertainty. Guilt!

Even Yosef knew that once hormones were in motion it was almost impossible to stop the train especially when none of the parties involved was willing to forfeit the thrill. He knew that he could have lost the position of the vizier if he had slept with his master's wife. As vain as the entire experience is, it abruptly ends at orgasm then reality sets back in and everyone counts the cost of something that cannot be reversed. Philip simply was not that strong. There was nowhere to run to, he was home, and the battle had met him there.

There were touches on the forearms, caresses on the belly, tickles and laughter. There was cuddling and squeezing, moans upon moans. Ecstasy beyond expectation as if the night would last forever. Clothes went off. Kisses were planted leaving the intoxicating taste of another gender's breath. The endless rush of hormones lasted for hours on end, six hours or more and Zainab could not take it anymore. She pulled away from him, utterly worn out. More exhausted from unsatisfied desire than the exertion all over the house - from the living room to her room and even to the washroom.... Why would Philip not go through with it. Why did he stop on the edge of such a boisterous river? Was something wrong with him? How could he hold back so much?

They had moved from the sofa to the floor. Rolled on the floor for hours. He had carried her to the bedroom, raising her expectation. Her top found its way far away from her, leaving her nipples exposed. Yet his manhood was intact. Erect but intact. How is it possible? How could he survive this attack? Did this make the sin any lighter for him? Was he trying not to sin too much. Was he afraid she might have a disease? He had even ventured to touch her in unspeakable places but only with his hands!

It was almost 3:00 AM. Zainab was away from him. She supported herself with her hands and knees on the carpet in her room, topless. He was on the bed, shirtless, stretching out towards her, hungry for more but guilt-ridden. The weakness of the flesh overwhelmed him. He wanted more but she had had enough. If he was not going to satisfy her, he had better stop arousing her. It was unbearable.

She reached for her top and pulled it over herself then she sat with her back against the wall. She was exhausted.

"Go and shower", Zainab whispered.

"Huh?" questioned Philip.

133

"it will make you feel better."

Philip paused, wondering to himself how many times she had done this sort of thing. It was his first, not counting those that had happened in his mind. It hurt him a bit the way she showed experience in sexual expression. He did not need experience, it was inbuilt, yet he felt inferior to her. She knew something about this new feeling that he did not know: it could be quenched with a simple cold shower. How pathetic! Why did he not quench it before it started?

In a few hours daylight would break, and life would be back to normal. He most likely would arrive at the office late. What would he say if someone asked what had kept him? Traffic. A lot of traffic.

The Day After

"Beloved, if our heart does not condemn us, we have confidence toward God." 1 John 3:21

It was such an awkward morning. Philip had never felt so unworthy. He had dressed up and sat on the couch in his chinos trousers and checkered shirt. He was not sure whether he was worthy of touching the Bible to have his morning devotion. As if Zainab heard his thoughts she came and sat beside him, brazen as far as he was concerned. She handed him a copy of the devotional and held the large Bible expecting him to read the day's portion. He was stunned but tried not to show it. She had her shorts on and a yellow vest that displayed her belly button. He read the devotion and she read the Bible passage. His prayer was shallow, unsure whether He was being heard.

Zainab had made him an omelette, she managed to wake up before he did. He woke up with her sitting by his bed, in his room. It seemed intrusive but pleasant on the one hand. Did she imagine herself his wife? Something was happening that he had little control over. He had opened a door he could not close quite easily.

"Are you OK"

"Yeah..." He answered without looking at her.

Silence.

"Thanks. I have to go. I am even late..."

He was explaining himself to her. The feeling of closeness between them was intoxicating but the heaviness on his soul was crippling. He had failed woefully, and he could not bring himself to turn around and ask for forgiveness. Some part of him wanted this to continue. How long could it possibly continue. His day at work was weird. There was a meeting later that morning and everyone smiled at him, but they seemed to be asking him what he had done the previous night. It was unbearable.

Helen had begun warming up to him again. She noticed the change in his disposition and wanted to know what was wrong. He obviously could not tell her. She pressed hard, hoping that being there for him in a time of need would be a good opportunity to regain his attention.

"Maybe he had broken up with that banker" she thought to herself.

"What are friends for? Let's talk now. We can talk over dinner or..."

She stared, waiting for an answer. Philip managed a smile. It did not mean what she thought it meant. He was wondering whether she would make such an offer if he really told her what he had been up to. She smiled back:

"So? Dinner?"

"Zainab... I mean Helen. Maybe another time. Don't worry about me. I will be OK. "

Helen froze. She was not fighting Abena. She was now fighting Zainab, probably a Nigerian. She didn't have a chance.

"Zainab," Helen signed, "I see. OK. I will let you be. But I am available anytime you would like to talk OK?"

"OK"

"Philip, I just want you to know that you need to think carefully about the people that really care about you. You need to know that relationships are really valuable. You are a full-grown man. You should know what is good for you!"

"OK Helen. I appreciate that."

Philip looked up from the computer screen he had been staring at and gave her a weak smile. She came close and rubbed his triceps. She looked straight into his eyes.

"You can call me anytime, OK?"

"OK"

At this point all Philip wanted was for her to go away. The following hour was quiet. the next intrusion was a phone call from Zainab. She had come to a restaurant near his office and wanted to have a chat with him. He obliged. It was a two-minute drive. There was hardly anyone at the place but the music from the radio made it hard to have a conversation in hushed tones.

Philip's first thoughts were "What is it that could not wait till he got home?". He underestimated the yearning of a woman for a lasting relationship. Intimacy to a woman is a perpetual experience. A woman could not experience one sexual encounter and not want another if she loved her man. As far as Zainab was concerned, Philip was her man, and nothing was going to change that. He let it go and sat down ready to listen. Even sitting with her in a restaurant felt awkward. He made up his mind that he was going to make sure the events of the previous night would never be repeated again.

"Hi!" Zainab started, smiling broadly.

"How are you?" Philip responded, trying to not get carried away.

"Are you OK?"

"OK as in?"

"I mean after last night?"

"What do you mean by OK?"

Zainab adjusted herself and her smile faded. She was not getting the kind of responses she had anticipated.

"I mean ..."

"If you mean is it going to happen again I can assure you it's not!"

The tone of Philip's voice was unwelcoming. Zainab wondered whether she had made a mistake in coming to him.

"Philip that's not what I mean. What do you take me for?"

"Zainab," Philip started. She leaned towards him and answered. "What we did was sinful, and we cannot afford to do it again. Do you realize that?"

"OK. I know. So, what does that mean? Do you want me to leave your house?"

"That's not the issue."

"I can leave your house and stay in a hotel until my house is ready. If that is what you want." She stared at him as if trying to read his true desires.

"I know we have sinned and all that, but I wish it doesn't change anything. I hope that we can still be as we were before all this happened..."

"As we were..."

"You know I think this happened because of all these feelings you have bottled up inside you. Sometimes you have to let it out. Let out how you really feel"

There was always something unsavory about Zainab's theology. Philip had lost touch with the Scriptures in recent years, but he still knew that feelings were not a good way to determine what was right. Feelings are transient, feelings are not to be trusted. Feelings can be used to justify one's failings, but they do not hold water in the face of eternal judgment. Philip knew this, and he so desperately wanted Zainab to get it if she really was the Christian she claimed to be. It was completely confusing. Did she even

139

believe in the existence of a God to whom she would be accountable? It was unfathomably puzzling.

The rest of lunch was particularly quiet. Then she left and then the silence spread through the rest of the day. There was a very queer aura around Philip at the office. He felt uneasy, not sad, not burdened with guilt to the point of mourning. He sometimes felt everyone knew what he had done because everyone seemed to look at him in a certain way. But how could they know, they better not know! He would lose all the respect he had in their eyes. He wished he could turn back the hands of time because it did not feel like this new passion of his would die out soon.

Just before close of business he decided he would speak to Gregory. Gregory Allotey was a very cheerful fellow from another department. He was very vocal about his faith and enthusiastic about sharing his faith with people in the office. He often told Philip about his evangelistic encounters whenever they chanced upon each other. Philip always felt challenged about sharing his faith more with friends and colleagues. Everyone knew he was a Christian, but he hardly ever directly urged colleagues to repent and be converted. They knew because he would not participate in certain discussions or attend the night clubs everyone was talking about or tell little lies to protect himself like his superiors expected. Philip however did do some apologetics, defending the Bible when those debates got heated, or defending his church when the journalists got naughty and features his pastor in the front page for talking too much about money.

Philip and Gregory sat in the small lounge where everyone received visitors on the first floor. There were comfortable upholstery chairs there and the television drowned their voices, making the conversation somewhat private just as Philip would have it.

"...I could not believe I was capable of this... but I am"

Gregory smiled when he finished. Philip did not expect that. What did he expect? Maybe someone who would scold him strongly about what he had done: living with a lady in the same house alone for weeks, almost sleeping with the lady, failing to take any actions to prevent a reoccurrence. Maybe some scolding would have made him feel better, but Gregory did not scold. He simply said, "Just pray, just speak in tongues..." That did not sound quite right. It first of all sounded very shallow, as if Gregory was not surprised about the Philip, a dear Christian brother, had done and just confessed to him. As Philip thought about it more it then seemed like Gregory himself must have been in the same or similar situation, as if it was something normal. His response did not seem like he was as horrified as a believer would have been ten or twenty years earlier. Maybe it was a Ghanaian phenomenon. Maybe every young Ghanaian Christian regularly had sexual encounters and simply 'spoke in tongues' for a few minutes to get rid of the guilt. Philip wasn't satisfied! He had to look for someone who would scold him about the issue. He decided he would call Amarachi or Emem. They certainly would have something strong to say about all this, they were women.

When Philip got home, dinner was ready. Zainab had proved herself to be a great cook. She had made White Rice and Goat meat pepper soup. Philip felt as if he was in Lagos. It was ecstatic, the meal. Then she brought the wine.

141

"Where did this come from?" Philip asked.

"Why? Do you have forbidden sources?" Zainab retorted without looking at him as she sat down on the floor leaning against the sofa. She filled two glasses and raised one towards him. He held on to it, a tinge of discomfort flooding his soul. She sipped hers, eyes on the television. The eight O'clock news was airing. Philip stared at her, smelling mischief. He also smelled something unhealthy in his glass: alcohol. He didn't know what it was, but he could tell if a glass contained alcohol by simply smelling it. Maybe everyone could do that, but Philip felt it was some spiritual gift God had bestowed on him with utter benevolence.

"Can I see the bottle, Zainab?"

"Why?"

"I want to know the contents, Ma!"

Zainab giggle and then answered softly:

"It contains wine…. Red wine."

"Do you realize you are grossly incorrigible? Why did you bring alcohol into my house? What is your plan? To get me drunk and have sex?"

"Philip!!! How can your mind be so dirty?" She sprang up feigning shock, "Is it five percent that you are describing as alcohol. So, five percent alcohol will get you drunk? Oh, *puh leeezzz*. This self-righteousness of yours is just unbearable!"

142

Philip stood up gently still holding the glass and walked to the kitchen. He poured the wine directly into the sink hole and opened the tap's faucet to clean it all up.

"Philip what are you doing? That's my wine! If you don't want it you don't have to pour it away. Just give it back"

Zainab had left her wrapper in the living room and was clad in her shorts and a purple vest. Her hair was wrapped in a hair net. She stood in the kitchen door, defiant, still carrying her own glass.

"Zainab please do not bring alcohol into my house! Please!"

"So, it is also a sin, right? Educate me"

"Just don't bring alcohol here. I do not want it"

"What is wrong with wine? Which Bible are you reading? Did Jesus not turn water to wine in your own Bible? Did the disciples not drink wine at the eucharist? Philip Ezeani, you are just trying to be more righteous than everyone else and killing yourself"

"What is your business with that? The point is I do not take alcohol and I do not want it in my house. I am not having a theological debate about it with you!"

Philip had dropped his cup and faced her, leaning against the kitchen sink, exasperated. What in all of God's green earth gave this young lady such boldness. Philip was beginning to see he had opened a huge can of worms with the excessive familiarity he had allowed with Zainab. She was gaining more and more control, almost manipulating him. He also realized he could hardly resist

143

her. Her legs were again apparent. Her cleavage. Her eyes. Even her defiance held an attraction for him. Then he felt the erection starting. Everything changed. Zainab could tell. Women can tell. He recalled an incident which made it obvious to him that they had some kind of sixth sense on these matters of the heart. Katherine Ehize was a very smart and pretty Nigerian-born Caucasian who had worked with him in Nigeria. He was attracted to her and was looking for all possible ways to express himself. On one of those days she made a statement to the hearing of everyone in the room:

"... I don't know how long Philip will stop staring at me from behind. Your eyes will not push me down o ...". All the ladies in the room had laughed. How could she have known he was looking at her when she had her back to him? Well she knew and now, Zainab knew. She knew he did not want her to leave the house. He wanted more of her even though his *Christian Personality* said it was sinful. Someone spiritual may put it another way: he didn't want this unhealthy relationship, but his *Carnal Personality* could not help it.

Zainab moved closer and stared in his eyes. She pushed him hard on his torso with her left hand, taking him by surprise. "Why did you throw away my red wine?" she enquired. He almost tripped but steadied himself with his left foot. She pushed him again. "Why?"

"Zainab, behave yourself! Are you OK?"

"Am I getting to you? Holy man of God?"

"You are very confusing. Or should I say very confused. Are you a Christian or not? What are you up to"

Zainab laughed out loud, clapping her hands twice. She put down the bottle of left over red wine on the kitchen sink right by Philip. She had her left hand softly on Philip's chest while she stretched her right hand to drop the bottle. Philip attempted to leave the kitchen, but she quickly grabbed him from behind with both arms, laughing loudly. Philip freaked out.

"What is wrong with you? Leave me alone!"

Their voices could be heard outside. Someone was listening. Zainab held on. He pulled her hands apart and she let go but before he could make another move she jumped and put both legs around him crossing them behind him. Her arms where around his neck and their heavy breaths touched each other's face. Philip hit her hard by the side pushed her legs down. "Stop it! Stop it!"

"Aawwww…", Zainab cried out and they stretched into a laughter. The play fight stretched for fifteen minutes and Philip's call for a halt got weaker and weaker till the encounter escalated into intense passion. All over the kitchen, into the living room till they ended up in bed around eleven thirty completely ignoring the TV which was still on and the bottle of half full red wine which was now being invaded by tiny red ants. Philip wasn't even sure whether he had locked the door or whether Zainab was an agent of the devil or whether he himself was still a Christian. In those moments of ecstasy, nothing seemed to matter. In the midst of it all he managed to keep his penis away from her vagina. The beads he felt around her lower waist line had scared him stiff. What was he dealing with here? Then in a few hours it was morning and they were lying beside each other.

145

"I am sorry…", Zainab said. Silence.

"I am sorry. I was drunk!" She kept talking.

Philip sat up on the bed and put both hands on the back of his head, hiding his face between his knees. "Father I'm sorry. Father please help me," he whispered. Even Zainab didn't hear him.

"Why are you unable to make love to me?

"What?" gasped Philip. He stood up and walked out of Zainab's room.

> *"I find then a law, that, when I would do good, evil is present with me. For I delight in the law of God after the inward man: But I see another law in my members, warring against the law of my mind, and bringing me into captivity to the law of sin which is in my members."*
>
> *(Rom 7:21-23)*

Guilt and Shame

"For godly sorrow produces repentance leading to salvation, not to be regretted; but the sorrow of the world produces death." II Corinthians 7:10

Philip was very regular at church. He had made good friends at The Accra Temple. It was a great church and he had been a member since the first week of his arrival in Accra. He wasn't in the work force though he had gone far with membership classes. Most of his friends were from membership class. Bishop Alfred Owusu was an excellent teacher. He held the entire congregation spellbound whenever he mounted the pulpit. The quality of his sermon delivery was consistently flawless; full of spiritual substance and very articulate. On this particular Sunday, however, Philip could not pay attention. His mind was fuzzy, ruffled by the events of the week. It had happened and was now part of his personal history. It could not be taken away.

After the service he and Zainab made their way to his vehicle outside the walls of the church premises. It was uncomfortable sitting by her in church. It was even more unsavory having to walk side by side with her in church. Everyone who looked at them seemed to be asking him "Who is this?". It was not Zainab's first time in church but today it seemed they had exchanged something that made this enquiry accentuated in the minds of those he had to say hello to. Zainab seemed to withdraw behind him each time he stopped to say hello to someone. She felt the rejection he was exuding towards her. She felt unwanted, like some kind of taint on his holy garments.

"Hi Philip..." it was Christopher, a gentle brother who had met him during the early days of his participation in the Church's membership classes. Christopher was one of those friends of Philip's who had married early. He was always intrigued by such brave men. He often wished he did get married on time. It seemed to be the Christian thing to do for a young man to get married in his early thirties. Anyone who failed to do so was bound to fall into some kind of sexual sin; mental or physical, open or secret, heterosexual or homosexual.

"Hello Chris. How are you doing," Philip replied, reaching out to give a handshake. "How was service?". He had to ask first, having hardly heard anything the Bishop said. It would have been dishonest of him to have answered "Fine".

"Church was great. Bishop simply cut through my heart with his explanation of Philippians 1:20. It's so challenging. Thank God for a man of God like him"

"Yes. Thank God"

That seemed a rather brief response from Philip on the day's sermon, but Christopher let it go. He took a glance at Zainab who was all but hiding behind Philip and decided to carry on.

"Alright Philip. Have to go... have a great week. One of these days you have to come over and eat some home cooked meal at my place"

Philip simply laughed. How could he tell his dear friend that meals were also being cooked in his home? One did not have to be married to get home cooked meals made by the delicate hands of a woman in his own home. And it was becoming more and more apparent that one did not need to be married to also get in bed with a young lady. But Philip could not say a thing like that, could he? It was completely unacceptable in this particular circle.

"Thank you" Philip concluded. He and Zainab went on.

"Your friend is nice. Christopher," Zainab started as soon as they sat in the Touareg.

"Yes. Very nice guy"

She looked at him. "You are ashamed of me. You didn't even introduce me to him"

"As what?" Philip asked himself.

"Sorry about that," he responded to her without looking. He accelerated.

Lunch was quiet. A home cooked meal. Philip was struggling with his thoughts, struggling with his integrity, his identity.

An hour later, Zainab had the pleasure of watching him iron his clothes for the week. She just stared, wishing he would say

149

something. He could feel the stare but held back for a significant period of time. Then spoke, just as he was ironing the last of five shirts.

"What are the beads for?"

"Beads?"

"The beads around your waist."

"Oh. Ha ha". Zainab gave him a long stare. "To charm you. I planned it from the moment I left Lagos. It is *Mammy Water* beads!"

Philip thought some of Zainab's jokes were very revealing, very suspicious. Sometimes he thought she was saying something to him that he should know but saying it in such a way that he would not know it.

"I am serious," he continued, "What are the beads on your waist for?"

Philip could not have known that many young African women wore waist beads given to them by their mothers for reasons that were not always explained to them. They kept wearing them even when they became Christians. How would he know? He had never undressed a lady before. It scared him stiff. Was she in some kind of cult? Had he exposed himself to demons with his sin? Could he ever get back to God?

"I don't know! My Mom gave it to me. But I hear it makes sex more exciting!" she laughed.

"I see. So, have you always worn it or did you plan to wear it that night along with the wine you bought?"

"Do you actually think I am trying to seduce you or something? Well, I am not. I didn't know what would happen. Can't you just be free and spontaneous? Why are you punishing yourself? Be free!"

"I cannot be spontaneously doing things that are clearly against God's will. I am not punishing myself. I am working on my ..."

"Can I ask my own questions?" Zainab interrupted, introducing a brief pause.

"I am listening"

"Why could you not have sex with me?"

"Huh? As a Christian shouldn't you be glad I did not? Could not! Why do you assume it is a could not rather than a would not?"

"Why would you not? OK. I know. Because it is a sin. *Duhh*"

Philip gave her one queer look and then stepped into his room to hang his shirt in the wardrobe. He took one last look to make sure it was smooth all over. He let out a deep sigh and then sat on the bed. Tears came close to his eyelids. It felt as if he was trapped. An hour later he was fast asleep with his back on the mattress and his feet on the floor: an uncomfortable position. He stirred gently; Zainab was sitting by him, rocking him gently.

"Get up and lie properly," she whispered.

"Hmm"

Philip stared at her for a bit. He wondered what she was listening to with her earphones. She repeated herself and he pulled his legs into the bed, and stretched, feeling the slight discomfort on his lower back that came with his initial position. He would certainly miss her when she would finally leave his house. Did she have to leave? Maybe they could get married. That would certainly be awkward. How would he give the testimony of their meeting among his plethora of spiritual brothers and sisters across the globe: 'God led her to my house and we lived together for a month and a half then He told me to marry her'? They wouldn't buy it for a pesewa!

Zainab sat by the bed for a little longer. One part of her wanted to lie beside him. Just to lie beside him nothing else. Nothing else intended. She stood up and went over to the wardrobes whose doors had been left ajar. She gently closed and locked them. Philip wasn't too deep in sleep to hear her. He was impressed, even pleased. She did know how to take care of a man. Zainab left him pondering, taking one last glance at her man lying carelessly on the large bed before she shut the door.

EXPOSED

Philip knew he had to talk to someone about what was going on. Every sin that remained hidden only festered and grew like dough injected with yeast. He thought about calling David Osiesaga. He would be so very disappointed. Maybe Olaolu Badmus, the one-time National Coordinator of his post-secondary school fellowship. He was significantly older and may be gentler on him. At work that week he had a chat with Gregory again and came very close to telling him that he had had another encounter with Zainab. What would he say this time? Maybe he would scold him. Gregory got a call into a meeting just as Philip was about to let the words leave the edge of his lips. It was extremely difficult, this confession thing, especially when he had to do it more than once. It would seem to whoever listened to him that he was deliberately repeating the same sin over and over again. How awfully embarrassing!

Amarachi called later that same evening. It was as if God was giving him an opportunity to deal with the issue. It was always such a pleasant experience chatting with Amara. He was so grateful Mr. Ade-Williams was the kind of easy-going person he was. Certainly, Amara must have told him he was once interested in her, but he was comfortable with her calling him every now and then.

"*Nwanne madu*[10]. How are you?" she started. Philip simply chuckled.

"You have thrown away your sister now"

"Ha ha. So, between you and I who threw the other away?"

"Brother *abeg* don't start. So, how are you? What have you been up to?"

"I am fine."

---

[10] Igbo expression literarily meaning "Someone's sibling". A way of saying "My Brother"

"You haven't answered the first question"

Philip burst out laughing hysterically. Amara always had amazingly witty comments that made him laugh and love her more. She didn't laugh much herself. She waited for him to stop before injecting another two or three similar comments.

"Back to the subject under consideration ..." she finally said, "What have you been up to? When are we coming to eat rice?"

Amara had great respect for Philip based on his past reputation, but she was also very sensitive. She had heard Ghanaian women were very aggressive and kept worrying about what Philip had been up to as a single person in a new environment. She was also extremely anxious to have him get over her completely and get someone else to marry. She felt responsible for his delay in settling down and felt it was part of her duty to push him into marriage.

"Any sister on board?" Amara kept pushing.

"Amarachi there is something I have to tell you."

She noticed the sudden tone of seriousness in his voice and her heart skipped a beat. Philip narrated his two encounters with Zainab over the phone while Amara listened intently for almost thirty minutes. She was in tears but did not let him know. Nothing changed about her voice, but she was in pain. Everyone ought to have seen it coming but everyone hopes it never comes. When a young man crosses thirty, thirty-five and keeps going it is only natural that at some point he will do something he did not plan to do sexually speaking.

154

"Well, so have you repented?" She asked solemnly.

"Yes."

"So where is the girl now?"

"Err... her house is still being prepared so she will move there soon"

"What do you mean by that? She is still in your house? What is she doing there? Philip this one is basic na! How can you live in the same house alone with a girl who is not your wife? It is totally unacceptable. You yourself have preached against that so why are you doing it? Because no one is watching? When is she leaving the house?"

"Err... "

"Philip are you telling me after two sexual encounters or whatever you call them you still do not see the need to have her leave your house immediately? The Bible says, 'If your right eye causes you to sin cut it off and throw it away'! You know what? I think you have become emotionally entangled with her and that's why you have not sent her away. Philip! I can't believe this"

"Amara slow down. I will tell her to leave. It's just that she doesn't have a place to go now because she is new in Ghana. She doesn't know anyone ..."

"Philip come on, these are flimsy excuses. You are exposing yourself to sin. Do not try to give it a nice name 'sexual experience' or 'sexual encounter' or whatever. Do not let Satan get the better of you. This has happened twice, but you need to deal with it and overcome and you need to be resolute about it so that it doesn't happen again. I hope you understand?"

"Amara but this was not intentional," He could tell she was really hurt by his failure.

"I know. I am not saying it is. I am just saying you need to be strong. Forgive me if I am sounding harsh but I really want you to find a way to make her go and live somewhere else. That is the best course of action. It's action we need now not just feeling sorry"

"OK..."

"Philip, I am counting on you. God is counting on you. You still have a lot of people whose lives you must impact so don't stay on this mountain too long. I hope you are listening?"

"Don't I get to speak?"

"I am listening, Sir?"

"Well..."

"OK. Please, don't drag the matter. Just try and get the girl out of your house and let's talk again. OK?"

"Yeah"

Philip's last response was like the squeak of a little mouse. He seemed to have got what he wanted, or what he needed: some good old bluntness. Amara respected him, but she was also one of those people who could tell him the truth to his face without batting an eyelid. He felt so ashamed that he now needed some bit of comfort. Who else could he call? Emem?

Airports. Everything about taking a trip by air was always worth looking to for Philip. The feeling of importance, the pleasure of meeting new people, the welcome part at the other end in MMA, Lagos. Everything was just ecstatic every single time. Philip had travelled to Nigeria about a week after speaking with Amara. It was a great relief to be away from everything for a while. He could actually leave the house for Zainab and was able to tell Amara that he was no longer in the same house as Zainab without telling her that he was not in Accra. He didn't consider it a lie, just a way of not telling the whole truth! From the back seat of a Red Cab he observed the structures on Oshodi-Apapa Expressway apparently speeding past him. Nothing had changed very much, same old Lagos: the heavy crowds of both vehicular and human traffic, buildings rubbing shoulders with each other, a major dual carriage way with one-foot deep flooded potholes at regular intervals. Same old Lagos. Philip's phone rang.

"Hi Stranger!" It was Zainab at the other end, excited as ever. "I just wanted to check that you arrived safely."

Philip smiled. It felt good having someone check on him, it felt bad that that person was not his wife. But then, Zainab could not be his wife. It was so complicated.

"Yes, I did"

"OK. I won't dry up your roaming credit... bye."

Philip smiled again and dropped the call. "I miss you," Zainab whispered at the other end. To her it was very simple. If he loved her he should say it. She did not want to be married to him necessarily, just to know that he loved her. God didn't matter, the neighbours or what they thought didn't matter. All that mattered to her was to know whether someone as special as Philip actually loved her despite her flaws. How could he get so close to making love to her and not make love to her? How could he be with her like that and not love her. She just could not comprehend it all. Her thoughts were on him all day while she did her rounds trying to get her new flat in order. She really didn't want to leave Philip's house. How would she cope?

Philip called Emem with a SIM card he had bought at the airport.

"Hello..."

"Hello Emem, it's Philip!"

"Hey! Charlie how far. Ghana man. What are you doing in our beloved country. Have you come to find a wife? Ha Ha Ha... it is well O. Will you be coming to the East? Are you..."

Emem never lacked words.

"Wait, wait, wait..." Philip interrupted, chuckling. He changed the topic and proceeded to gently narrate his experience with Zainab to Emem. He felt some kind of relief telling other Christians about his failings. The apostle James wrote to the Hebrews to confess their sins to one another and Philip felt that it was the right thing to under the circumstances. To him it seemed the act of confession helped him to shed the shame and guilt he constantly felt even after enjoying his sexual encounters. Emen listened intently unlike her. It was definitely a shock to her but not out of this world. She just didn't think Philip was that kind of person.

"But why did you allow her to stay with you in the first place?" she asked. This seemed to be the famous question of cause. No matter how sophisticated Christians become or have become, no matter how Pentecostal or how massive the grace revolution becomes, everyone still knows that living with the opposite sex for a protracted period will eventually result in fornication of one form or another. Grace never takes away our humanity, it merely covers its effects and relieves us of the eternal consequences of our sin. We are spiritual beings, carrying a very physical body about in a very physical world.

"But thank God you did not have sex o. It would have been worse," she said. Emem had never been shy about calling the word out over and over. Sometimes Philip thought she got emotional high by mentioning 'sex'. She continued:

"Philip do you know that some girls are just devilish. They can just give themselves a target to bring down someone, even married men. Someone can see you as you are now and feel that since you don't even send girls, they want to show you they can bring you down. See, one of my colleagues eh..." Emem went on and on with tale after tale of similar men who were conquered by ladies not married to them and trapped into marriages or with pregnancies. Philip was always amazed at the number of tales of this nature she

159

was privy to. He just listened and responded at intervals until he got to his hotel in Festac Town.

Philip had deliberately opted to stay in Festac Town because he needed to sit with Wole Adelaja, a veteran of his secondary school fellowship whom he respected very much. He spoke to him about the issue upon his visit to his house, he was milder, telling him how perception of the boundaries of relationships differed from person to person based on their upbringing.

"Before I got married," he started, while driving him back to his hotel, "on my twenty-seventh birthday, Amaka said she had a surprise for me. She asked me to close my eyes and I did. I tried to cheat though and noticed she was coming closer. Before I knew it, she had planted a kiss on me, mouth to mouth. It was brief though, but I was shocked. It didn't mean anything to her though. She did it with a clear conscience. So, some of these grey areas, they actually depend on upbringing..."

For Philip, having someone speak in this way was soothing but he still had doubts that this described his scenario. He was not in a relationship with Zainab, so he could not compare with Wole's case. Besides, the response of anyone who heard his side of the story would depend on the details he managed to give of what actually took place between him and Zainab; for him it was a very difficult story to repeat.

The Other Side of the Story

Zainab assumed her position as *Madam of the Ezeani Residence* during Philip's week out of town. She had begun mingling with friends from her university and some were coming home with her in groups, both male and female. She was never one to refrain from fraternizing with anyone who was willing. She simply loved affection; she didn't feel emotionally bound to any one not even Philip. She was free. She got introduced to Erobosa Enebuwa very quickly during one of those times when they had to make payments at the bank and they both caught on to each other very quickly. Erobosa was the typical Nigerian diva from Benin, Edo state. Reckless, carefree, naturally smart, stunningly attractive but totally uninterested in any form of romantic relationship with even a tinge of commitment. She just wanted to have fun with life. She had managed to convince Zainab to let her visit on the next Saturday. Their time together was ecstatic for Zainab, she laughed her hardest during their conversations then it got serious.

"So, do you love him?"

"Love who?"

"Mother Teresa! Philip in whose house thou livest in sin! Hahahaha"

"Oh, get serious!"

"That's not an answer..."

"Babe, forget that side"

"Oh, see your face don turn red o. You love him. Well, I wish you well. Hope he loves you too. And how is he in bed?"

"What?"

"Oh, please get real, Zainab. Share with me! I have experience! I can help you. Ha ha ha ha ha..."

Zainab was surprisingly embarrassed. As sanguine as she was, she wasn't really accustomed to speaking about her sexual experiences with such casualness. Such discussions brought up memories of her past which made her withdraw. There was so much hurt hidden behind the sunshine of her smiles; hurt that had created within her such restraint that it was amazing how easily she fell into Philip's arms.

She was only eighteen when she became the victim of a scandal in Kwara State Polytechnic, Offa. Her Philosophy professor had trailed her to her flat off campus on several occasions and finally walked into her room on the first floor of a private hostel through an open door. She was shocked and excited at the same time seeing him in her room. It was about 5:30 PM, she remembered clearly because she had just finished watching a series on television while cooking. Three hours later, one thing led to another and the Professor shattered her hymen amidst suppressed screams. Nobody came to her aid. Screams of ecstasy were nothing unusual in off-campus hostels. Most students who chose to live off campus were either running away from the crowded hostels or were actually running towards the utter freedom to do and undo without the disturbance of the likes of Campus Fellowship preachers. Outside campus, the Cult Boys were the kings and the girls were available. Nothing was amiss, she was simply enjoying the encounter as far as everyone who heard her scream was concerned. The professor left in his well-known Mercedes 500 E vehicle and three weeks later his wife came and put up a show in Zainab's neighborhood, naming and shaming all the girls her husband had been with in the same building where Zainab was living. She could not stay there any longer, but the experience stayed with her.

Then there was her secret lover, a boyfriend she could not introduce to her parents because they were relatives. Up to three times he had slept with her in the family house. The entire arrangement was emotionally paralyzing but she simply could not break free from him. It was like heroine, drawing the addict back to itself over and over again, threatening to kill him with withdrawal symptoms whenever he tried to break free. Drugs and sex were similar kinds of slavery: the master was fun to be with, the master was in control, the master always left bitterness of soul after each encounter.

"He's ok" Zainab summarized looking innocently at her new friend in the face. She preferred to spare the gory details of the *almost sexual*, all-over-the-house encounters she had with Philip Ezeani. She gave Erobosa that look that made it clear she did not want to continue the conversation along those lines. The diva ignored the stare.

"How many orgasms?"

"What? Ero you are so spoilt! Sinful! Ha ha ha ha ha!"

"Oh, forget that thing. We are all sinners. That is why Jesus came! If there is no sin, there is no grace!"

"Erobosa please I don't want to talk about it"

"I can help you o. I have this special viagra eh ... And maybe we can even do a threesome. What do you think?" her eyes widened as she spoke.

"Erobosa stop! Are you crazy?"

"Ha! Girl it's OK o. You can keep your man. I just wanted to help o. No hard feelings. In fact, I want to start going sef..."

The look on her face spelt disappointment. Something was not right about this. Did Erobosa really have this threesome matter as an original plan? Completely unheard of. As scandalous as the suggestion was, what made it any different from sleeping with a fellow one was not married to? Or practicing homosexuality? Or bestiality? Or playing with sex toys? Masturbating? Casual kissing? The list goes on and on. Who makes the rules about where the

164

boundaries are? After all every single one of these sexual expressions is an attempt to satisfy a genuine human desire. Who draws the boundaries as to what expressions is not allowed in a single person's context? If a threesome is abhorrent, why are other expressions not so abhorrent? Or more abhorrent? Is there some kind of grading for these sexual sins based on severity? Who grades them?

Erobosa left and Zainab was by herself again. She walked to the room and picked up her violin, locked the front door and sat inclined on the sofa, knees curved with feet on the sofa, playing to herself. Her thoughts then began to reel.

"What is really wrong with a threesome? I have slept with three men, I am living with one and we have done just about everything except actual penetration! What has suddenly made me become Sanctified Mother Mary? I might as well just do it! Maybe it will be fun"

"Will God ever forgive me? Why does he have to? After all He was watching when it all started. I am hurt. I don't even know the way back or how to stop any more. It's just not my fault"

"I wish I could find someone who would help me. If only Philip could have helped me. Now he can't even help himself. He was supposed to be the 'Holy Brother' wasn't he? Now we are the same!"

"What am I even going to tell Hassan. Hassan? Why am I even thinking about him? One of my biggest problems in this life!"

The tears trickled down through her lower eyelashes, messing up the mascara and down her cheeks leaving a rough trail on her facial. She didn't wail, she didn't even sob but she was deeply hurt. The tears kept coming until she slept off.

Shocker

"For she has cast down many wounded, And all who were slain by her were strong men." Proverbs 7:26

Sunday Afternoon. Philip was ready to return to Accra. Hassan had promised to pick him up but he was a little delayed. Calls kept going back and forth between them till they agreed to meet at Festac Extension near Oshodi-Apapa Expressway. Philip boarded a motor bike, carrying his travel bag on his right knee. The Lagos life in him was still intact!

"*Fatgbems*! Fast please!"

The reckless rate at which the Motorbike rider rode his bike through Second Avenue, Frist Avenue, Apple Junction all the way to the express made Philip wish he never made that second request. But he didn't rescind, he just prayed under his breath that he would meet Hassan in one piece. He paid the rider just before he jumped off the bike. In seconds, he was running across the dual carriage along with other pedestrians to meet Hassan in his Toyota Corolla. He was ready to move quickly, already facing the correct direction. Philip caught up with him and promptly threw his single piece luggage in the back seat.

"Wow! Thanks, Hassan," Philip sighed as soon as he was seated in the front seat. It was a relief to be once again shielded from the hustle and bustle of Lagos by the rolled-up glasses and air-conditioned car. He strapped his seat belt and he couldn't help noticing Hassan chuckled. Philip knew why the chuckle came but Hassan proceeded to announce:

"We no dey tie belt here o. This is Lagos!"

Philip burst out laughing.

"'This is Lagos'. You just reminded me of that joke. When coming from the East to Lagos by bus, every state you pass through gives you a nice looking welcome message. 'Welcome to Anambra', 'Welcome to Delta State', 'Welcome to Edo,' ... But when you get to Lagos it looks more like a warning: 'This is Lagos!'".

Both men roared with laughter.

"Seriously I am not even sure whether I can live in this city again," said Philip.

"Why ke? The stress? No be stress o, na hussle! No let Accra make you lose your hussle o. Because if person no get job wey dey pay am monthly im still need that hussle. Living in Lagos is great training my brother. You can survive anywhere"

"Interesting. Well, if that is the case, it should be the most prosperous city in the world. Why must we think making things extremely difficult is a great way to train people? Are we moving forward or backward?"

"Oh' boy, if people for US or UK get the kain corrupt leaders wey we get here, dem go just dey die anyhow for those countries. We are still here because as a people, we get hussle and when it comes to hussle, Lagos is d main d main o. Na di blessing wey we get be dat!"

"Survival. If we keep hustling and surviving decade after decade, we are not developing. How long can things be like this. Why are there eighteen million people in Lagos in the first place? Because nothing significant is happening in any other city of this nation. Is that how to run a country? With proper thinking, people will not need 'Hussle Training' to make significant strides in life. Let's change our way of thinking"

The discussion went on and on from jokes to politics to football to women then to Zainab. The conspicuously missing topic of discussion was spirituality. Philip could not even discuss anything close to spirituality. He couldn't even discuss religion when Hassan mentioned something related from his studies of the Haddith. They were already on the stretch leading up to Murtala Muhammed International Airport when Philip began slowly breaking the news of his encounters with Zainab. He would not keep it in anymore. After every round of laughter, his conscience seemed to resurrect with more vibrancy. It would have been utterly dishonest of him to keep the issue a secret from his friend who trusted him enough as a committed Christian, Born Again and Spirit-filled, to let his female cousin stay with him for a few weeks in a foreign country.

Zainab had warned him very sternly not to say anything to Hassan. "Why?" he had asked repeatedly and emphatically to which she would respond "Why do you have to? What do you intend to achieve by doing that?" or something similar. The aggression with which Zainab resisted this proposition of his was very suspicious. Philip could not understand it. He even quoted the Bible to her:

"He who covers his sins will not prosper, but whoever confesses and forsakes them will have mercy" Proverbs 28:13

Zainab would not budge. She warned him he would be responsible for whatever happened to her as a result of his telling Hassan about their 'relationship'. She called it a relationship, but Philip certainly didn't feel like it was a relationship, he felt like it was a sin they had to be set free from. Relationship? Every encounter he had with her seemed to make the whole scenario diminish in purpose. He knew very well he had no intention of marrying her, did not love her as a person even though he was definitely sexually attracted to her and was not comfortable with the circumstances of their 'relationship'. He just had to find a way to end it.

Hassan listened to him elaborate on what took place one line at a time. Hassan asked questions and he responded honestly, getting some relief that he was finally getting this done, feeling lighter as he confessed. He was grateful for Hassan's understanding, he even hoped he would gain the respect of this Muslim friend of his by coming clean. Then they came to a stop at the Airport Car Park and stepped out of the car. The atmosphere had changed between them. Philip understood; it was bound to be disappointing to Hassan.

Philip stepped out of the car wishing there was something he could do to relieve his dear friend of the pain and reduce the tension, but he just could not think of anything. He couldn't look him in the eye after this and Hassan was unusually silent. He helped drag Philip's luggage out of the back seat. He dropped the wheels on the floor and began pulling it alongside Philip towards the departure gate.

170

Philip noticed he kept his face as hard as a flint, eyes straight ahead of him. He heard the click of his car keys locking the doors electronically. Apart from that there was no other sound between them till they got quite close to the departure gate where the Immigration officers asked for the passports. Philip took the box from Hassan and dipped his hand into the side pocket to pick his passport, he always kept it there, considering it much safer that his trouser pocket.

As soon as he opened the data page he felt the sudden hard impact of a clenched fist bouncing off his face just beside his left nostril. The knuckle hit so hard that it cracked the layer of soft skin inside his nostril and he began bleeding. He had fallen to the floor and his passport booklet was at least two feet away, his black jeans were decorated, with a patch of white dust from the airport floor and he found himself resting on his elbows, partially dazed. His retina was blurred partially by the effect of the knockout. He wiped his eyes and sat up, briefly observing the immigration officers holding Hassan back who was yelling at the top of his voice:

"You are a fool! You mess up big time! I say you mess up. Bastard!!!"

"Wetin be dat?" asked one of the officers while Philip was still in shock, "No be your friend?"

"Dis wan na woman matter," laughed the other officer, "Im done go service im friend wife!"

"Gentleman do you know where you are," the first officer chided Hassan, "You want to be arrested?"

"Horrific!" said a certain plump middle-aged lady who had been in the line behind the duo. She helped Philip get up, being careful not to expose her behind, her dress being somewhat short. She almost toppled over on her two-inch high heels. Philip ended up steadying her and their eyes met. "I am so sorry" she apologized on Hassan's behalf, "He is such a jerk! What could you have done to him?"

She had a strong welsh accent though she was a complete negro. Philip couldn't tell whether she was actually Nigerian. She must have been. He raised his head from her face and was embarrassed to see the crowd staring in his direction from across the street, inside the airport buildings, everywhere. He quickly dusted himself and picked his luggage saying absolutely nothing. The lady trotted behind him, helping to dust his jeans from behind.

"Oya, abeg let me go," Hassan said to the Immigration officers. He sounded calmer then. They let him go and made more comment about what warranted such a sudden turn of events between friends.

"If I know I for capture dis thing for video o. YouTube money for come today o. See punch!" said the second officer, triggering a round of laughter from those who heard him. They watched Hassan walk briskly back to the car park.

"Next please…" called the first officer.

Amanda Okoro ended up sitting beside Philip on the flight. She managed to convince the senior citizen whose seat it was to switch seats with her. Philip was happy to have good company. What harm could be done. Besides it was soothing that someone was concerned about him after that huge shock of a punch.

"You live in Accra?" Amanda started. She adjusted the hem of her dress trying to pull it further towards her knees, but it only ended up attracting Philip's attention to the exposure. She sat by the aisle and the fifty plus gentleman in glasses on the other side of the aisle had his eyes fixated on her laps.

"Yes, I do. You?"

"I do rounds every quarter. London, Lagos, Accra, Abidjan. Hectic!"

"Wow. A lot of travelling. Must be exciting"

"Oh no! You get fed up with it after a while. Life's ever so unstable. Can we switch? I kind of fancy the window, you know"

Philip thought her smile was manipulative. She had moved his seat partner now she was moving him.

"So, what happened with your friend?" Amanda asked after she had moved over him to the window seat. "Why did he punch you like that?"

Amanda kept her eyes on him, but he only glanced at her every now and then as he responded. The conversation went on and on until Philip ended up sharing his dilemma with Amanda Okoro, a complete stranger. He ended up stating that he did not in any way expect such an extreme reaction from Hassan. He thought it had been forgiven in the car. "Brothers look out for their sisters…" Amanda had offered.

The conversation switched from personal issues to professional issues and about fifty minutes later they were exchanging cards at the Arrivals hall of Kot oka International Airport with a promise to meet up as soon as possible. Amanda left first, and he watched her wondering where this was headed. She was obviously older, so he felt somewhat safe.

"Surprise!!!"

"Hey! What are you doing here?"

It was Abena.

"I am here to pick you up. Let's go!"

"Heerrr... have you been stalking me?"

Abena laughed. "Well, I went to your office and they told me you were on your way back today. You have dumped me now, so I came to see you myself. Mohammed and the mountain!"

"Hahaha... no... been busy."

"With which one? Your Nigerian girlfriend, Ghanaian girlfriend or the one at the office? By the way I have made up with Helen o. I told her we are just friends. We almost came together in fact"

"Serious. I am impressed"

"So, who is your new girlfriend?"

"Who?"

"The lady you were talking with"

Abena walked briskly towards her car and Philip trailed behind, wondering why she was in such a hurry.

"Hahaha. You think everyone is my girlfriend now? "

"Ok. Your beloved not your girlfriend"

Philip startled some passersby with the roar of his laughter. Abena wasn't amused. Philip noticed how serious she seemed and tried to explain without giving details of what led up to their acquaintance.

"I just met her on the plane. We happened to sit together"

"I see…"

"I haven't been on a plane outside Ghana before but whenever I go to Tamale by air, whenever people get to their destination everyone goes their own way. I scarcely see people walking with the people they sat with to arrivals!"

"Hahaha. Abena are you OK? You are sounding jealous!"

Philip had just dropped his luggage in the open booth. He walked to the passenger side of the front seat as he made the last statement. Abena was on the driver's side. She stopped and stared at him momentarily.

"You mean jealous of you flying in planes every now and then?"

The look on her face was a warning that this line of discussion was no longer safe. He changed topics.

175

"Nice car" he complimented, shutting the door at exactly the same time as Abena started the engine. He was always proud of his upwardly mobile career lady friend. The rest of the drive was not very eventful and as soon as they reached *Ablekuma*, Abena declined following him in. Zainab came towards the window as soon as she heard the sound of the small red *Kia Venga* stopping by the gate. She didn't see clearly but it was obvious Philip was being dropped off by a young lady.

Back in the car Philip reached out to hug Abena and she obliged. This was a little rare between them. They held on for a few seconds then Abena pushed him away abruptly when she felt his lips on her neck!

"What? Are you OK? Did you just kiss me? What? I can't believe this!". She kept shaking her head and expressing disgust with the gestures on her face. Philip was dumbfounded. Why did he do that? He had no idea! He just stared into space while Abena questioned him with her eyes. He was glad she resisted at the same time surprised that she, whom he did not think of as particularly spiritual, was the one who woke him up. Abena was raised in a staunch Catholic family and morality was very important. Virginity was a strong virtue. To Pentecostals of the twenty-first century, Speaking in Tongues was much more important than virginity. To Catholics, it was different. There was pride in keeping oneself intact till marriage. Philip experienced the reality of that conviction from Abena's response. She knew exactly where the boundaries were.

"You see you...", Abena continued her scolding, "You need help o. Please get out of my car!"

Philip promptly opened the door and stepped out. He managed to pick his luggage from the booth and came back, peeping through the glass to say goodbye. "I'm sorry" he mumbled but Abena zoomed off without responding. He pulled out the trolley handle gently and walked through the gate which had been ajar, dragging his bag and a heavy dose of depression. Something was wrong with him. He needed help.

Zainab opened up the front door and beamed with a smile, bright as sunshine. Her eyes sparkled and looked straight into his. She hugged him hard and she took his travel bag from him bringing it through the door.

"Great to have you back" Her voice was ever so soft. "How was your trip?"

"Great! God has been good. Thank God for journey mercies"

Both were smiling sheepishly and blushing heavily. To Zainab, it felt just like welcoming her husband home. She shut the door gently and locked it while Philip looked at her shorts which she had worn specially for this moment. He smelt the mild feminine body spray. When she turned around and look at his eyes again she knew he was ready for her. She pulled him towards herself and planted her lips on his. He did not resist. The entire cycle repeated itself again and they were in bed with each other at 7:00 PM after a few hours of sleep.

"We did it again!" Zainab started.

"Hmm"

"Why don't we just accept that we are in love?"

Zainab chuckled.

"This is not funny Zainab!"

Zainab was seated in a fetal position on the bed while Philip was on the edge.

"There is a cut on your nose. What happened to you?" asked Zainab softly. Philip hesitated.

"Hassan"

"Hassan?"

"He hit me at the airport after I told him"

"After you told him. After you told him what?"

"About us..."

"Philip!" she gasped, "I told you not to tell him. I told you not to tell him. Oh God! What have you done? You have ruined my life, Philip, you have just made my life more complicated"

"What is he going to do? Tell your parents? I didn't feel comfortable hiding it from him. My conscience wouldn't allow me; I just had to let it out. Zainab, I don't know whether you realize it but we are living in sin..."

"You and who? Look Philip, sin is a personal thing. If you think you are living in sin that's your business! Leave me out of your holiness craze. Oh God! What have you done?"

She paused then started wailing all over again. Philip stood up to leave but she sprang up and pulled him back. He stared at her, shocked.

"What is it?" he asked, "Let me go and sort out myself with God since you have no problem with this arrangement"

She pushed him on the chest and yelled loudly, "You are a fool, Philip! You are a fool! You don't even know what you have done"

Philip was flabbergasted. This was way out of line coming from a lady he let into his house. It appears letting someone into one's bed comes with consequences. He was utterly confused, bereft of words. "Zainab, behave yourself! Behave!" Her eyes widened, defiant. He pushed her away and made for the door again, but she pulled him back. That was when he turned and threw a slap which narrowly missed her left cheek. He heard her mutter the 'F' word and gasped. She repeated herself, much louder.

"Yes! I said it! Do you worst. You have already done your worst. How about CNN and BBC?" She cried, and let loose the bed sheet with which she had been covering herself, "You can even take my nude pictures and post on Facebook so that God can forgive you. Nonsense!"

Philip walked out and went towards his room. She followed. Zainab kept talking, voice raised:

179

"And in case it hadn't dawned on you, Hassan and I have been together! Many times!"

Philip turned back and stared at her for a moment. He wanted to say something, but he had no idea what he could possibly say. Should he ask whether they were really cousins? Should he ask how long ago this was? What was the nature of their relationship? Was it real sexual intercourse or merely the kind of encounters they had been having? He just did not know what to say. He turned back and went into his room. From behind the door, he could still hear Zainab's voice:

"Yes, Philip, someone made love to me. I am worth it! Someone had the courage to come into me. I am a woman, Philip, I am ..."

Then the sobbing started, and she went back and slammed the door shut behind her. She threw herself on the floor and sobbed till midnight.

> "Do not look on the wine when it is red,
> When it sparkles in the cup,
> When it swirls around smoothly;
> At the last it bites like a serpent,
> And stings like a viper."
>
> Solomon, Israel's Wisest King

Forgiveness

"If we confess our sins, He is faithful and just to forgive us our sins and to cleanse us from all unrighteousness" 1 John 1:9

Some of the *holiest* and most respected men whose lives were recorded in the Inspired Scriptures carried the peculiar burden of the most jaw-dropping sins; dastardly unspeakable acts of profound wickedness. We speak of things we fail to sufficiently cringe and cry out about because we are simply reading them not watching them happen in the graphic detail of real life. We do not know whether the first man Adam was eventually reconciled to God but if indeed his error plunged the entire human race into the danger of irreversible eternal perdition, ever increasing degrees of callous wickedness, the indescribable pains of thirty-nine classes of disease, catastrophic inexplicable holocausts, sinless bloody wars of accentuating proportions decade after decade, and the several other discomforts of this present world, then we need to ask with all sincerity, *Is Adam worth forgiving?*

The error of Abraham gave rise to a man named Ismail. The prophecy about him was that his hand would be against every man and every man's hand against him. It could well be that if the spouse-sponsored sexual encounter between Abraham and Hagar had been excluded from history, there would be less than half the terrorist organizations there are on earth today and maybe nil in the Middle East? Israel as a nation would be living in absolute peace with her neighbours, the likes of Al Qaeda, Al-Shabaab, Boko Haram and ISIS would be non-existent. Palestine would have an entirely different landscape. If we are to tread strictly on the path of absolute justice, we cannot help but ask: *Is Abraham worth forgiving?*

Dawud was well known to be the man after God's heart, one of the greatest kings of Israel by conquest. His fame spread throughout his generation as a champion of faith starting from his victory over a giant probably twice his height. He was the most loved king of Israel, turning distressed, in-debt and discontented fellows into mighty men of valour. Even today, Dawud is a significant reference point to Jews, Christian and Muslims, yet in his moment of idleness, what was initially an unwise act in search of fleeting pleasure, a temporary sensual, visual gratification grew into an adulterous affair of weeks, and eventually into a carefully planned murder, executed right at the battlefront when the king discovered the woman was pregnant. Uriyah was a foreigner but he was obviously more disciplined and more committed than Dawud to Israel's victory in that battle and thus died in it. *Is Dawud worth forgiving?*

Solomon, Israel's wisest king, went way beyond the Old Testament boundaries for kings by having sexual relationships with one thousand women of different creeds, religions, nations and social backgrounds. He started out well, asking for wisdom rather than wealth yet receiving wealth of unimaginable proportions from the Giver. With his gift intact, he plunged his nation into the path of idol worship incurring divine wrath and eventually division and judgment for Israel through his multiplicity of idol worshipping women. Yet in the twenty-first century, we read his books, and covet his wisdom and wealth. *Is Solomon worth forgiving?*

Philip's private contemplations had reached the point where he asked the same question about himself. *Was Philip Ezeani worth forgiving?* He knew all there was to know about sexual purity, he had taught others on setting boundaries, and he had seen all the signs long before he found himself repeatedly entangled in Zainab's arms. Was *he* worth forgiving? Locked away in his room by himself he began running the previous few months' events through his mind: the first call from Hassan, the day he picked up Zainab from the bus park, the night she played music for him, the first encounter, the night he couldn't even utter a word of prayer when she fell ill. Who would he be praying to? A God he had so terribly disappointed? He just could not get himself to look in His face. Would God even listen to him? It seemed to him a severe case of hypocrisy to be praying for Zainab if the subject of the prayer was not how to get help out of the quagmire he had sunk into since Zainab came into his house. This time however, he knew exactly what to say.

> *"Lord, I have failed so woefully. I cannot even believe it myself. I cannot understand how I got this far. I missed it when I let Zainab come here. I am so sorry. I wish I had insisted on telling Hassan 'NO'. I don't even know what to do. I cannot believe how nasty this has become. Even Hassan has slept with her. I am so sorry. I wish I had never let this happened. And look what I have become, even with Abena ... so shameful. I am so sorry Lord! Please forgive me. 'If you should mark iniquity, who would stand?'. Help*

me to be strong. Help me to stop repeating this sin. I am so sorry. Please take distractive women away from my life. Take Zainab away, take Abena away, take Helen away from me. Lord take all these distractions away from me. I want to live for you. Please help me to be strong. Help me to honour You with my life."

Philip spoke to God for almost two hours, praying and crying. The emotional burden on him was heavy. He wanted a radical change that evening. He wanted to be free. He wanted to be restored to the spiritual state he was known for before he arrived in Ghana. He wanted to be confident about preaching the Gospel in public again. He wanted his reputation restored. He wanted to be able to tell those who looked up to him for spiritual guidance back in Nigeria that he lived an upright life abroad. His prayer was heartfelt and intense, and he did receive forgiveness, forgiveness is free. It is given as soon as it is requested. There are no prerequisites for forgiveness except the simple, sincere request. He did hear the Voice though, the Silent Whisper. It had been ages since he heard that soft nudging voice in his heart.

"Three questions for you, Philip: One. Are you more concerned about Zainab's forgiveness than about yours? Two. What bothers you most? Your reputation or your relationship with Me? Three. How far can you go to ensure that you do not repeat this error?"

A week later Philip went through interviews to join the Ushers in Church. Following the interview, a senior member of the team took special interest in him. She was in her fifties, a single mother of a fifteen-year-old girl. She had never been married. She had the most vibrant personality Philip had ever encountered and they got along very well the first time. Philip felt she could help him and he was willing to express himself more freely with her.

Within the same week Zainab left the house to stay at a cheap hotel till her house was ready. It was a shock to Philip when he came home one night and found she was not there. They hadn't spoken to each other much since the last quarrel that followed the last sexual encounter. But he couldn't afford her absence just yet, especially at a hotel. He still felt responsible for her and Hassan was due to arrive in Accra that same week. He did not want Hassan to come and find out he had left her to go and stay at a hotel in a strange country, almost as if Zainab was a little girl. But then, Hassan had sort of handed her over to him, hadn't he? He dropped his office paraphernalia and dashed out again. As soon as he started the engine he realized he didn't know which hotel she was at. He dashed back into the living room and picked up the note she left which he had not finished reading. *Magenta Hotel.* He knew that three-star hotel, it was near the Gazelle West Africa head office where they had met face to face for the first time a few months earlier.

Zainab was so hard to predict. Philip did not know what to expect but he certainly didn't expect the simple smile she had greeted him with as soon as he came through the room door. It seemed to be a smile of victory, as if she had expected him to come looking for her. She had proven something to herself and maybe to him.

"Come. Sit down!" she beckoned, still smiling like a secondary school girl who was being wooed. Philip stared around the unsophisticated hotel room. There was nowhere decent enough to

185

sit except the bed. He obliged, keeping what he thought was a safe distance. She looked into his face.

"What can I do for you?" she asked rhetorically, still smiling, tight-lipped this time.

Philip pondered briefly on the question. It was a good question? Why did he come here? What did he want from her? To come back *home*? Maybe he should simply have let her be. She continued talking, adjusting her scarf, tightly wrapped around her scalp.

"You said I was making you sin so I decided to leave your house so it can be sanctified!"

Philip did not know how to respond to that but he attempted.

"Hassan is coming. I do not want him to get the impression that I sent you out"

"So, Hassan wants me to come back to *your* house, right?" Zainab giggled.

"How long do you intend to stay here. This house of yours in *Agyirigano*, when will it finally be ready?"

"I can take care of myself, Oga. Even if it's one month, I will foot the bill! Why are you bothering yourself? I don't want to tempt you anymore now!"

The game went on and on: Philip refusing to tell her directly to 'come home' and she was trying her possible best to make him accept that he wanted her back. That he missed her. That he loved her? Eventually she simply sprang up and went for her luggage in the wardrobe. She had hardly unpacked. And it was just some hand luggage, in the note she had let him know she would return for the rest when her house was ready. Philip helped her with the small box, paid off the bill for the night and soon they were back home. It felt like bringing one's wife back home after a nasty quarrel, like some kind of makeup was necessary. Then the atmosphere changed again, like it was the first night she arrived. Like it was the night he came back from Nigeria. A similar sequence of event unfolded and in three hours, they fell asleep in each other's arms, both topless, both spent from exertion, both burdened with guilt yet not wanting to leave the bed. Philip's bed. And the Silent Whisper was silent.

Philip couldn't muster courage for another prayer for forgiveness. He just let things be as they were. Somewhere down in his heart he feared that his conscience could be growing callous. He wasn't feeling it anymore, the heaviness in the aftermath. It began to feel normal, something natural, something necessary. Hassan understood. He even asked him whether he loved her. Philip didn't answer. Hassan spent the week in Accra in the same room as Zainab. Often on those nights Philip would hear the sound of giggling and wince. It would have been so much more straightforward if they could just let things flow and not feel the need to repent. Just before Hassan left, he helped Zainab move to her new apartment. Philip could not believe how much she acted as if she did not know him from Adam. At least that was how he felt. Hassan's presence seemed to change the atmosphere dramatically. But why was he hurt? He had no claim on her, did he? He ought to have been elated that someone was taking away the source of his problems. It was all such an emotional roller coaster.

Voices from the immediate past kept ringing in his head. Voices that had spoken about these *near-sex* experiences with Zainab Audu Garba.

Emem: "... Some ladies just give themselves a target to bring a man down. It's like an oath, once they are done they have won!"

Lara: "Ha ha ha ha. You! Claiming to be virgin, after all you have done. *Which kain virgin be dat?*"

Amarachi: "Look, if your right eye causes you to sin, cut it off and throw it away. Philip cut that girl off and throw her away! It may hurt but that's what you need to do."

Wole: "... it often depends on upbringing. Some ladies don't see kissing as a breach of the boundaries..."

Elder Onuzo: "... no matter how many times you sin, each time it happens, make sure you pray and repent. The Lord will give you grace..."

Zainab: "I will haunt you! Even in your dreams I will haunt you..."

His thoughts were broken twice by two calls that Saturday evening as he spent the time completely alone the first time in a very long time. The first call was from Amanda Okoro, the second was from Helen Eduful. He picked neither. He was already having enough issues. The next day he managed to catch up with Miss Botchway and her daughter after service and they had a long chat as he narrated his story again with much discomfort and shame. He did leave out the gory details and especially left out the fact that he had repeated the sin just a few days earlier. It was too shameful.

"The way you give these accounts, I get the impression that you believe it is all Zainab's fault", she commented. Philip stared at her slightly wrinkled face. She smiled gently and continued:

"You didn't say so but that may be how you feel. You are the holy one and all the ladies are targeting you because you are well of. That may not be the case you know"

She allowed him to ponder over her statement then added, "I wish I could speak with her too…"

"And you must realize Philip, that there is a world of difference between a request for forgiveness and actual repentance. We can ask for forgiveness and be very emotional about it. We cry and wail and make promises and pledges but the very next day we repeat the sin. It is called a besetting sin. The primary way to deal with it is radical repentance. Sometimes radical repentance means removing permanently the source of our trouble even if it hurts deeply! Remember what Jesus said, 'If thy right hand offend thee, cut it off…', Let's read it… Matthew five twenty-nine."

She pulled out her Bible and opened the passage.

> *And if thy right eye offend thee, pluck it out, and cast it from thee: for it is profitable for thee that one of thy members should perish, and not that thy whole*

189

body should be cast into hell. And if thy right hand offend thee, cut it off, and cast it from thee: for it is profitable for thee that one of thy members should perish, and not that thy whole body should be cast into hell.

"Imagine the hurt if we actually had to literally pluck out our eyes when they looked at something unhealthy on TV for example. Or if we had to cut off our hands if we used them to hurt someone or steal... that is the vehemence with which Jesus wants us to throw away things that cause sin. Let's assume you even love Zainab, you cannot build a lasting relationship with her given the events that you have narrated to me. It's not a good foundation. You must let her go!"

Miss Botchway's manner of speech was ever so soft. Even when she used strong terms she didn't raise her voice or strain herself. Her emotions were very much under control. Her tone indicated such firmness but you could never accuse her of being rude or judgmental. Whenever she spoke the name of Jesus, she spoke very affectionately, like he was standing right by her and paused for half a second like his name brought a memory of having seen Him face to face.

"Mummy are we going yet?" asked Naa. She called out from a distance. Her Mom and Philip had been leaning against their car for almost forty-five minutes. Philip smiled, feeling for her. He excused himself and walked over to his own car and set off for home.

He thought about Miss Botchway's demeanor on his way home. She reminded him of someone. Yes! She really did pass for an older version of Mrs. Ade-Williams. He was sure she would turn out as a sound counsellor as she aged. He imagined they would still be great friends wherever she was, wherever he was, and whomever he was eventually married to.

Repentance

"He who covers his sins will not prosper, But whoever confesses and forsakes them will have mercy."
Proverbs 28:13

Two weeks passed, and Philip went through the routine of waking early, going to work and returning to an empty house. The routine slightly changed when he went to church on Wednesdays. He seemed to be getting a bit more regular at the worship services. He had spoken to Abena for three weeks either, just a few lines of text on WhatsApp. Helen was always there, smiling at him in the office, making jokes he rarely laughed at. No calls from Emem or Lara but Amara called to ensure Zainab was no longer in his house. Once again in his life in Accra, he was for all intents and purposes alone.

After service on the second Wednesday, he got chatting with Miss Botchway again.

"I know once I get married, all this will go away…"

Miss Botchway laughed softly. "That is not necessarily true. Paul did say it is better to marry than to burn but marriage is not the solution to sin, Jesus is"

"Are you saying marriage will not help me get over my weaknesses?"

"Marriage is not just about sex, Philip dear. And think of it like this: if you have never taken cold water and you take it for the first time, you will want more. If you lack control when you do get married, being married will not magically make you contain yourself. Self-control is a battle that must be settled before one gets married. Sex with one person will never satisfy you in this world without the help of the Holy Spirit. And you do know that the fact that we are not having literal sex does not mean we are sexually pure in God's sight. Sexual purity is first and foremost mental."

"Very thought provoking. Very scary"

"Yes"

A relatively long silence ensued. It gave Philip time to think. Could he survive another fifty years on earth without sexual sin? He had made it to his late thirties without the actual sex act, but like Lara mocked, he had no right to call himself a virgin. He was way past that. He noticed Miss. Botchway glancing at her watch. It was almost 9:00 PM and her daughter would call her anytime soon.

Miss. Botchway looked around the auditorium. It was full of soft, deep blue seats in perfect array forming an incredible pattern if one could take an aerial view from those expensive flood lights hanging from the roof. It was full of seats now but almost empty of people. The last batch of ushers went to and fro and some turned off the air conditioners. It was almost time to go.

"Philip," Miss. Botchway called, breaking into his deep thoughts, "Let's take a walk outside..."

She breathed heavily as she stood up. Philip reached out to help her but hesitated. He would rather avoid touching her. There was something that excited him about older women who managed to keep their youth whether it was by being contemporary in their dressing or expressing significant intelligence. It was more intense when they happened to be single or their husbands happened to be absent somehow. He wasn't so sure whether it was really a sexual attraction. It could not be! But it was certainly some kind of attraction. He had developed such an attraction for Miss. Botchway in such a short time and she had observed it but she was very much in control. As they walked out side by side to the exterior of the thousand-seater church auditorium, she spoke up again:

"Philip,"

"Yes, Madam?"

"How would you describe the difference between forgiveness and repentance?"

"Well, forgiveness is what God does to us when we repent!"

Philip sounded very academic in his response and Miss Botchway smiled lovingly. She even glanced at him. It was a smile easy to misconstrue if the discussion had a been a different one.

"That is close to the truth. But you know, God forgives us when we ask for forgiveness not actually when we repent."

She reached for her phone and read first John chapter one verses six to ten:

"6 If we say that we have fellowship with Him, and walk in darkness, we lie and do not practice the truth. 7 But if we walk in the light as He is in the light, we have fellowship with one another, and the blood of Jesus Christ His Son cleanses us from all sin.

8 If we say that we have no sin, we deceive ourselves, and the truth is not in us. 9 If we confess our sins, He is faithful and just to forgive us our sins and to cleanse us from all unrighteousness. 10 If we say that we have not sinned, we make Him a liar, and His word is not in us."

Philip knew this scripture by heart. He had prayed extensively with it many times. Often when he quoted it, he did so aggressively and passionately, trying to convince himself that God had actually forgiven him for yet another near-sex experience with Zainab or some other young lady. He knew that God would forgive but he could not tell for how long God would keep forgiving. The other scripture in Hebrews chapter ten verse twenty-six often jumped at him making it difficult to accept God's forgiveness after so many failures.

"You know Philip," Miss Botchway started again, ever so gently, "The first part of the passage tells us that we cannot remain in fellowship with the Father while walking in darkness. The second half, verses eight to ten, tells us that we can get God's forgiveness simply by confessing our sins. Once we accept our sin, confess and ask forgiveness, our fellowship is restored. It is very important to do this as quickly as possible because it keeps us out of Satan's reach but ... but, what is more important is dealing with sin to the extent that we are no longer repeating it"

She paused and breathed heavily. She remembered her own sins. Like the Jews who dropped their stones at the feet of Jesus when the adulteress was pardoned, she had found in her own life that it was always easier to understand and forgive others whose sins were similar to one's own. She had lost count of how many abortions she had when she was much younger, many of them years after she had confessed Christ as Lord and Saviour. She knew what it meant to deal with besetting sins. She knew what iniquity was.

"Let me say one last thing before I leave you. It's getting very late. In fact, I am surprised Naa hasn't called yet. OK. Philip, when I was young, I had a Pastor who was very patient with me. When he could not take my repeated failures anymore, he told me what the Bible meant when it said '... iniquity was found in him...' referring to Lucifer. He said that our acts of sin are symptoms, sin itself is the common denominator among all men, the nature that Jesus came to take away. But iniquity can be thought of as a flaw in our beings that manifests in repeated acts of sin. It could be anger, sex, theft and so on. A manifestation of something rooted in us that God needs to uproot. Often, we have to take drastic actions to have that iniquity uprooted. Let's get back to the subject of repentance. To repent is to turn away from something decisively. The interesting thing is that while forgiveness is His part, repentance is our part. We must go beyond repeatedly asking for forgiveness to actually turning away from our sin. Drastic actions are often required to make this happen in us. God is not powerless to deliver us but we must position ourselves correctly and demonstrate that we are willing to be influenced by His Holy Spirit in a permanent way. I hope you understand?"

Philip nodded.

The ride home was full of deep thought for Philip. He knew what he had to do. He had to go and apologize to Zainab and let her know he no longer wanted to blame her for all his failures. The iniquity was in him, he did not need to blame someone else for his own failures. If Zainab wasn't there, someone else would be. Maybe Lara, or Emem, Abena, or Helen .... It was just a matter of time and opportunity, anyone of them could have been a victim of his own iniquity. She didn't have to feel it was all her fault. He had to go and apologize and make things right.

It was a noble thought he toyed with for another week and then placed a call. She sent him her location on Google Map and he drove there from work the following Friday evening. He felt an unhealthy excitement, there was an eerie silence all over him that evening, but he went anyway. An hour's drive, the traffic along Achimota Highway was jaw breaking as usual. Those travelling to Nsawam and beyond competed with those who had built their houses at Pokuase, Amasaman, Kuntunse, Medie and all along the way and of course the roads were bad.

There was a power outage in Zainab's new area. It was rare in Adabraka and Zainab reminisced on her days in Philip's house. Things were a bit easier. She certainly couldn't afford a three-bedroom flat and certainly not a large compound like Philip's.

Living alone wasn't much fun either so she had to keep inviting her friends to stay over especially Erobosa. She never stopped tickling Zainab's imagination with all her escapades. Zainab missed Philip. He couldn't have showed up at a better time that Friday evening – she was lonely, it was dark and she sat in the dark having no use for the lamp, she was not dressed for visitors, just her shorts and vest. The weather was so hot she would even have sat naked if she could. She had no idea Philip would come around so when she heard the knock on the door she opened eagerly, desperate for company. Their eyes met and she muttered "Hello" but turned back into her one room self-contained apartment, leaving the door ajar. Philip took that as an invitation to enter. He hesitated. "Why are the lights out?" He asked, almost as if they had been on talking terms all the while. As if nothing had happened. As if Miss Botchway never existed. As if he had lost touch with his memory. Zainab felt as though they were starting over where they left off.

"Did you see light in any other house when you were coming?"

Philip chuckled.

"I mean don't you have a lamp or something?"

He kept standing but she had settled back into the single chair that decorated the living room.

"Please sit down," she offered, "I don't have any chairs so you can use the beanbag"

Philip looked around, and caught the rechargeable lantern on the reading table. He turned it on and then sat on the wooden chair. He found it too hard so he took Zainab's offer and sat on the beanbag. The rug was quite thick, he observed. He imagined she often slept in the living room rather than walk into the adjoining bedroom. He could see part of a large mattress lying in the room through the translucent curtain tossed gently back and forth by infrequent bursts of breeze.

"So, what brings you here?"

Zainab didn't look at him. She seemed to be staring at the wall, easing her discomfort with a hand fan.

"I thought we should talk," Philip replied.

"About what?"

Philip hesitated. He was on the verge of saying 'About us' but thought it might create the wrong impression even before the discussion started. Zainab stood up gently and sat beside him, on the soft rug, leaning against the wall.

"So, what do you want to talk about?" She asked again.

She curled up in a fetal position, pulled her shin in with her forearms and laid her cheek on her knees; eyes raised looking into Philip's face. She strained to see the expression on his face since the lamp was behind him. He saw her face quite clearly. Her eyes reminded him of many things that had before then begun to sink into his subconscious.

"I just wanted you to know... I want you to know that I don't blame you for everything that happened when you stayed at my place..."

199

Philip watched a gentle smile form slowly on Zainab's face. The blush that mixed with this smile made her look exceptionally attractive. It felt like there was music playing, a soft wind gently passing by, a solemn moment. It changed everything that he had planned for that evening. A little cuddling followed. Then a lot of cuddling. Philip left the house about two hours later. It would never seize to amaze him the amount of time he could spend with Zainab saying nothing in words but expressing much emotion.

The mattress was on the bare floor but quite comfortable with Zainab in it with him. Everything seemed quiet and no one seemed to be watching. When it was over, his eyes stared at the ceiling as Zainab laid on his chest. It dawned on him: the difference between forgiveness and repentance, the iniquity that was inside him. It wasn't Zainab's fault, neither Helen's nor Abena's. It wasn't even Victoria. The iniquity was inside him and he had to take responsibility for it. He had been forgiven too many times now he needed to turn his back on all this. There was no need to cry or to pray another set of long prayers. What he needed to do was clearly revealed. He needed to cut this arm off completely and bleed.

At 1:00 am he sat up and prepared to leave. Zainab stretched and ruffled the already unkempt bed spread.

"Are you leaving?" She asked, her voice sounding worried.

"Yes please"

Zainab sat up, a little confused. In the brief silence, they heard the chirping of crickets outside. The light of the full moon filtered through the blinds carving their shapes in the otherwise dark room. Philip stood and pulled his T-shirt over himself. He took one more look at her and then turned to leave. She followed. As she got to the door she spoke again, almost desperate.

"Will I see you again, soon?"

"No, Zainab. No. I'm sorry"

She cringed.

"OK"

She heard the door shut as Philip left. She somehow knew it was all over. She would never see him again. There was something very decisive about his answer. It was the last time. She took one step forward and gently locked the door. Nothing more needed to be said.

Epilogue

Two years later. Miss Botchway was busy packing her small leather bag. She went back and forth around the house looking for one thing or the other. She glanced at the clock and exclaimed "Hei!" every now and then. She was running out of time, almost a little worked up and not her usual self. The phone rang.

"Oh! Who could this be at this very wrong time?"

She reached for the mobile phone on the dining table and touched the surface. She saw a long number starting with +97.

"What country is this?" she asked herself just before she picked.

"Hello Aunty Anita!"

The voice was unmistakable. And only one lady in the world had such a ring in her voice and tinge of pure excitement when she called her name. She chuckled.

"Hei Zai ... nab! What part of the world are you in now?"

"I'm not telling ...."

"Hmmm... secrets from Aunty Anita, huh? So, how are you?"

"I am fine Ma. What's your shoe size? It was supposed to be a surprise, but I can't afford to miss it"

"Ha ha ha ... 'Surely the Lord God does nothing,

unless He reveals His secret to His servants the prophets.' I am blessed. I wear size ten. Big feet!"

"Ha ha ha. Ho ho ho. OK. Watch out for my surprise soon"

"Thanks very much, Zainab. God bless you, OK. I am grateful you thought about me wherever you are"

"Welcome Aunty Anita. I love you so much"

"I love you too, Zainab. I have to rush now. Philip has asked me to come over and help take care of his baby girl"

"OK. That's so nice of you, Aunty Anita. My regards to them. I will talk with you later and reveal all my secrets. Take care of yourself. Mmmuah!"

"Bye, Zainab."

The End

Appendices

In this book, Njànsí, the main character, is a young boy who returns to his family and the real world after inadvertently dabbling into the occult through an encounter with his supposed Spiritual Guide.

Being previously assumed dead, he now stands in the middle of a long spiritual battle for his own soul between his family and the occult. Maureen, Njànsí's Aunt, finally gets him out of the occult but not before he establishes his own order.

Till Death explores the marital journey of Emeka and Modupe Eluigwe, an intertribal Christian couple who navigate life together through the ups and downs of marriage. The book explores the effects of pain, unfaithfulness, children and even age on the marriage institution.

Till Death is narrated by a mysterious entity who watches the couple from start to finish and draws the reader's attention to such matters as the purpose of marriage and the concept of judgement.

Kenneth Igiri's books are available in bookshops in Ghana and Nigeria as well as on Amazon. You can keep in touch with him on the following channels:

https://www.youtube.com/c/KennethIgiri

https://www.facebook.com/scribblingsage/

https://twitter.com/kenigiri

ABOUT THE BOOK

Philip Ezeani, a middle-aged single Christian finds himself in a roller coaster, undefined relationship with an unintended live-in lover, Zainab Audu Garba. His life is further complicated by the myriad of women in his past and present who have taken up various positions in his heart, unknown to them and often unclear to him. Philip finds himself unable to control himself and finally discovers that his life has not been hijacked by external forces but by something living inside him.

Based on a true story, *Entangled* tells explores the concepts of sin and forgiveness, sonship and slavery, lust and love. A young man finds himself failing over and over because he has failed to accurately analyze his true strengths and weaknesses. He fails because he has not taken time to be honest with himself. The filth hidden within his heart is suddenly exposed, embarrassing him, trapping him, enslaving him. He has judged others without first judging himself, oblivious of what he was capable of until he was exposed to the right (or wrong) set of circumstances.

ABOUT THE AUTHOR

Kenneth is a Nigerian Christian of Igbo extraction based in Accra, Ghana. His books tell stories from an African/Christian point of view and they are very original inviting the reader to analyse faith and societal concepts as they are subtly expressed in each storyline.

When not writing, promoting entrepreneurs or in church with children, he can be found playing with Oracle, SQL Server or MySQL Databases. He is passionate about his job but definitely finds creative writing a significant part of his life. He has two other published works, Njànsí and Till Death both available on Amazon as well as in bookshops across Lagos and Accra. He also maintains a blog www.scribblingsage.com which covers a variety of thought-provoking subjects and excerpts of his books.

Kenneth is happily married to Joycelyn, a beautiful and soft-spoken Ewe lady and they have a little baby boy, Shemaya.